Walter Octavius Peile

West of Swardham

Vol. III

Walter Octavius Peile

West of Swardham
Vol. III

ISBN/EAN: 9783337047412

Printed in Europe, USA, Canada, Australia, Japan

Cover: Foto ©Andreas Hilbeck / pixelio.de

More available books at **www.hansebooks.com**

WEST OF SWARDHAM

A Novel

BY

THE REV W. O. PEILE,

AUTHOR OF "TAY."

IN THREE VOLUMES.

VOL. III.

LONDON:

HURST AND BLACKETT, PUBLISHERS,

13, GREAT MARLBOROUGH STREET.

1885.

Bungay:

CLAY AND TAYLOR, PRINTERS.

CONTENTS

OF

THE THIRD VOLUME.

WEST OF SWARDHAM.

IT was the harsh and hurried sound caused by dropping anchor which first roused John West to consciousness that the voyage was over. So soundly had he slumbered that he has since suspected the Count of having administered some sedative or opiate ; but, be that as it might, he felt on awaking that he was himself again, such as he had been before that terrible night which seemed already to belong to

the dim past. Spite of his still distressful
plight, the strong man rejoiced in his
recovered vigour. Come what would, it
seemed good to be alive, even in absolutest
destitution, while a sunbeam flickered
through the port, and the aches and pains
of the last few days were no more than
troubled dreams, gone with the darkness.
He was soon on his feet, and peering from
the port-hole.

Could this be Bergen? Why, it seemed a
solitude, a background of rocks and fir-trees
at no great distance from the yacht, and
rising sheer from the same dark waters on
which she rode. Hark! there was a boat
approaching ; he could hear, but did not see
it. Looking round the tiny cabin he caught
sight of a suit of tidy blue serge, a striped

shirt, and other toilette necessaries, disposed where they would meet his eye. Oh, the rapture of it!—here was a truce to the worst of his destitution. He was not long in clothing himself, and not long in tumbling up on deck, full of curiosity as to his whereabouts. No one took any notice of him for a while,—for the crew were busy with their visitors, whose boat with its enormous oars floated alongside,—and he stared with all his eyes around him.

Not a trace to be seen of the German Ocean!—the yacht lay in a land-locked channel half a mile or less in width, of whose steep sides, rocky and fir-crowned, he had spied a sample from his port. But at a little distance there was a bay, from which the stony barrier retired in a fine sweep,

leaving room for a sward or meadow of the
most brilliant tint of green. That flowery,
grassy nook seemed to John West as fair
a sight as he had ever looked upon. In
places on this beautiful expanse of herbage
there were clumps of birches, in others
patches of cultivated ground whence crops
of oats or rye had been cut. Near to the
water's edge were two or three wooden
houses, all gaudily painted, close to which
was a much higher and larger building, of
fanciful and pagoda-like appearance, likewise all of wood. It had many gables,
from which projected the roof ridges in
great grotesque finials, arching outwards
like outstretched arms. In the centre rose
a sort of gabled turret, with a flag-staff.
The whole edifice, except the ground floor,

was covered with wooden tiles, looking at a little distance like scales, and painted in several shades of green. Further back, upon a knoll studded with Scotch firs of such beauty as to rival Italian pines, stood a venerable but almost shapeless pile of ancient stone, which seemed half ruinous. In the remoter background more than one waterfall descended from the heights, tumbling in successive cascades that showed white among the sombre spruces. The Englishman scanned all eagerly, marking with a sportsman's eye the capabilities of the country.

'I don't see a salmon river,' he thought, 'but otherwise I should consider this place a paradise for four months of the year. Is the count a sporting character, I wonder!'

He looked to the stern, where Bjornsen and
FitzRaymond were engaged in reading the
letters brought to them by the shore-boat.
For the latter but one letter had been delivered, but this seemed to have excited him
considerably. He had seized on his friend,
ruthlessly interrupting his perusal of his
own correspondence, and now the pair were
in earnest discussion over the open sheet.

'I could fancy the skipper shooting
pretty straight,' Jack thought; 'but as to
my compatriot, I should be very sorry to be
within range of his gun. How he shakes!
What a brute he looks, considering the
smart chap he once was! I am not at all
anxious to renew acquaintance, and neither,
apparently, is he.'

There appeared, by the gestures of the

two men, to be some dispute or difference between them, arising from the letter which both had read. Violence on the part of the colonel produced only the usual shrug of the count's shoulders. He had said his say, and at last stood contemptuously aloof while the other, haggard and excited, bustled into the boat which straightway made for the shore. The count stood for a while looking after the retreating oars with no very amiable expression, and pulling his black moustaches. Then he caught sight of Jack, and moved towards him with a quick, bright smile.

'Welcome to Bjornestrand,' he said, in his low pleasant tones. 'I rejoice to see that you are so far recovered that I can do the poor honours of the place.'

Jack bowed and smiled in return, feeling as much drawn to this man as repelled by the other.

'Honours,' he said, 'are no due of mine. You have clothed the naked and fed the hungry, whose life you had first been the means of preserving.'

The count stopped him with a gentle laugh and wave of the hand.

'No gratitude is due of mine. There are those of your countrymen who would certainly feel none, and I rejoice to have been of any slight service to one who, I am sure, deserves the best efforts. Let us talk of other things. Is this your first sight of Norway? Yes; well, I wish it were a more enchanting view. Ah! you find it not without a charm! But this is but one of a thousand fiords—featureless and poor compared with many—no show-place visited by travellers. Yonder you see the crumbling ruin of the old tower of the Bjornsens, with the few acres that alone are left to us in these days. You wonder perhaps what is that grotesque edifice nearer to us' (he pointed to the green pagoda). 'It is a sort of parody of one of our old churches—probably ancient parodies in their turn of Byzantine architecture. But that green monstrosity is no church. Alas! it is a summer-house—an inn without customers, a folly of my poor father, who thought to rival the Sogne or Hardanger here, and built a house for tourists who seldom did him the honour of approaching it. Now and again in the summer season

it receives a stray traveller; on rare occasions
a party will steam up our fiord; but it is a
monument of failure, that sole attempt of
the Bjornsens to be enriched by commercial
enterprise.' Again he laughed pleasantly. 'At
any rate it can offer better accommodation
than the chilly vaults of our poor old dungeon
there, and such as it is I hope you will be
my guest in it as long as you feel disposed.'

Earnestly Jack thanked this good-natured
fellow for his hospitality, and then went
on to say—

'I must be a burden on you only till I
can devise a way of earning my bread once
more. Perhaps you can help me to this?
I will do anything that an able-bodied
fellow can undertake.'

'Then you do not desire to return at

present to England,' the count asked, looking attentively at him.

'You would not wonder if you knew
my case that I have no wish to return to
England.'

'Perhaps I know more than you suppose.
Fortune has used you badly. You have
been hurled, by no fault of your own, from
a proud position to absolute poverty ! You
see that I am informed, no matter how,
of your past. What lapse of time and slow
decay has accomplished in the family which
I represent, one hour brought about for
you. I was ten years your junior when I
began my battle of life, as penniless as you,
and I have never gone under; nay, I have
trampled on those who scorned me sometimes; never have I been trampled on !

And are you—*you* to resign yourself to slave
and drudge among sons of the soil? No,
you shall not. Rather cast in your lot with
mine! Listen, I will speak freely, for I
feel I may trust you. I am disappointed,
I am disgusted with FitzRaymond. My
only desire is to disembarrass myself as soon
as possible of this man without self-control.
Let him end his miserable life in floods
of the brandy for which he would sell his
soul; I am done with him. But in you I see
the possibility of such camaraderie as I desire
—you would be the ally for whom I seek.'

Warming as he proceeded, the count
urged this most unexpected proposal with
much vivacity. Though touched by an
offer of fellowship so surprising, Jack was
not a little bewildered. What was the

proffered position ? In what fashion was the count's mysterious battle of life conducted, which involved some trampling on prostrate foes ? Still gratitude so far prevailed over hesitancy that his answer was not displeasing to his host.

'Ah, yes,' said this latter, 'you will have leisure in this dead and silent place to know me better. I will unfold to you my plans for next year—my campaign against the enemy ! And when you weigh what I can offer—a life of travel, adventure, society —against the lot of a mere toiler among toilers, you cannot hesitate. Come, the boat returns for us , let us make for the unwonted joys of terra firma, including, perhaps, even a dessert of multer-berries and cream after our *déjeuner*.'

In the course of half-an-hour Jack found himself at table in a fairly spacious room, ceiled, floored, and walled with deal, and furnished after the plainest fashion of a provincial *salle à manger*. The fare was likewise simple, consisting mainly of fish, fresh and salted, eggs, and oatmeal porridge mixed with cream. These humble delicacies were served by a young woman in red bodice and double snood of the same colour. FitzRaymond took his place at the board. but, as the count observed, neither ate much nor made agreeable conversation for those who were eating. West could feel no surprise that his host should have wearied of ' the colonel,' who was rude and insolent, almost ignoring the third guest, and coarsely abusing the viands, especially the rye bread.

which was indeed of a startling black colour. It appeared that he was extremely ill-pleased to have been delayed by his friend's hospitalities, for he kept demanding a conveyance for Bergen.

'I ought to be there, or half way at any rate, by this time,' he cried angrily, 'and you keep me in this cursed hole, though you know what is up, and what suspense I'm in.'

The count answered always with unruffled equanimity, assuring his irritable and uncivil guest that no horses for the land journey were to be had, and that the person into whose presence he was so anxious to rush would undoubtedly arrive very shortly at Bjornestrand, thereby saving him all fatigue.

'Pray resign yourself,' he continued:

'have a little faith in me, a little consideration for the peculiarities of my country. Be content, and take a cup of this excellent coffee.'

FitzRaymond seemed to regard the coffee as a mere excuse or vehicle for ample additions from a flask labelled 'Trondhjem Aquavit.' It was horrible to see how his eyes glared at the spirit, with what frightful intensity of craving he demanded more and more of it, spilling his coffee into the saucer, and hoarsely insisting that the cup should be filled brimful from the brandy-bottle. Jack was moved to pity amid his loathing for the man. Good heavens! what was the deepest descent from riches to penury, what was the abruptest turn of Fortune's wheel, compared with this abyss of degradation into which he, who once seemed a gallant gentleman, had precipitated himself?

The meal concluded, FitzRaymond began restlessly to pace the gravel in front of the door, bending his blood-shot eyes on a point at the head of the fiord where he supposed that persons approaching from Bergen by land would first be visible. His haggard lips were working, his fingers twitching. He was evidently a prey to an excitement which had blotted from his mind all interest whether in Bjornsen or in the man whom he had recognized as of 'his own county.'

Leaving him to his own devices, the count set himself to do the honours of his patrimony to his new friend. First they strolled through some other chambers of the pagoda-like building, all alike finished in

wood and scantily furnished, of which one
had the fittings of a bar, with barrels and
bottles ranged on shelves behind. The
windows of the upper rooms opened on to
small balconies, whence were gained pretty
but not extensive views up or down the fiord.
Next he led his guest across the beautifully
green sward to the ruinous old tower, and
showed its melancholy rooms, with their
rudely vaulted roofs and windows admitting
a minimum of light. These were the only
dwellings, save two or three peasants'
houses, on the property, and these were
well-nigh deserted. More to Jack's taste was
the out-door aspect of the place—the copses
where they flushed the Norwegian grouse,
now exchanging its darker summer plumage
for delicate French-grey tints, soon to fade

into pure white at the near approach of winter; the brooks that promised trout; even the marshes, where some children were busy picking the 'molte-beer' (multer-berry or cloud-berry)—a fruit twice as large as our bramble-berry, and of yellow instead of jetty dye. He wondered how the owner of all these things, the descendant of the builders of that mouldering tower, came to be such as he was—an accomplished citizen of the world; a slight, slim figure dressed in well-cut clothes, fitter for Cowes pier than for this northern solitude.

For hours they rambled on, enjoying the free use of their limbs after the narrow limits of the yacht, and engaged in pleasant talk, which was a wondrous treat to Jack, so long cut off from the society of cultured men. The count was full of interesting detail, of stories and legends respecting his country, its customs and antiquities, its fiords and sounds, mountains and inland lakes. And he talked well, showing that he could be a charming companion in the presence of an intelligent being, silent and curt as he had been with the sottish Aylmer FitzRaymond. Amid the glories of a magnificent sunset he conducted his guest once more into the low vaulted hall of the old tower. A huge fire of fir-logs and cones blazed on the ancient hearth, and on the rude table of black oak a simple re-fection was set forth—flad bröd, resembling oat cake, salt butter, cheese, and cured salmon, and a bottle of claret. With these and some excellent cigars the pair regaled themselves, and then, sitting in the gathering gloom on logs covered with reindeer skins, chatted on before the blaze, with increasing good fellowship. After a while the count's easy flow of talk turned on his own personality—mentioning incidentally that his mother had been a French-woman, and that his boyhood had been spent at a Parisian *lycée*.

'From my paternal line,' he said, 'I have inherited little but the roving instincts of the old vikings; I have travelled much, and, if it has been after a fashion singularly unlike a voyage in the long keels of yore, I too have spoiled the Southerner at times. I have humbled the insolence of the rich on that fairest of fields, greener and more level than the ground we trod just now—the

board of green cloth, the modern battle-
field, round which gather Egyptian and
Hebrew, heroes and birds of prey.'

The man's eyes lit with unholy fire as he
made this vaunt ; for a moment they rested
on his companion, and then gazed outward
down the darkling fiord, as if yearning for a
sight of some illuminated fairy palace reared
by the blue Mediterranean to harbour the
accursed rites of which he was a devotee.

Mute and sorrowful the Englishman
turned away from the man whom he had
begun to like. A gambler, perhaps an
unscrupulous gambler, even a card-sharper !
—such then was the wretched explanation
of his hints as to his feud with the world ;
such was the vile profession in which he
had sought a new partner. And this was

the true character of the man who had
spoken of honest manual toil as if it
could sully, nay as the most unspeakable
degradation !

Doubtless he had marked for his own one
whom chance had flung into his hands
naked and penniless—one whose rearing
unfitted him for labour, while it would
make him a valuable associate in the pur-
suit of human prey. Could indignity go
further than this, that to him, the son of
Rachel West, should be offered the post of
decoy, of accomplice, the ' bonnet's ' share in
the plunder of the free-lance his chief! It
revolted him to owe anything to the charity
of such an one as stood revealed in this
Eric Bjornsen ; and yet the clothes he wore
were his gift, yet he had eaten of his bread ;

yes, and he had felt the attraction of the man, and still acknowledged it to such degree that he could not despise him as utterly as he had despised his sottish colleague. But he would be beholden to him for nothing further—he would not sleep beneath his roof. On foot and alone he must make his way to Bergen, and there seek for employment. He had risen and passed through the doorway into the night, leaving the court to his day-dream of Monte Carlo; but now he turned back, and accosted him, as he stood lost in thought, in cold constrained tones, more suggestive of the proud young squire of Swardham than of Jack Wood the fowler, the castaway.

'If I have rightly conceived your meaning,' he said, 'I ought at once to say that there is no calling so humble, no way of life so mean and poor, that I do not prefer it to the most successful, most luxurious career that ever fell to a gambler's lot. It pains and grieves me to appear ungrateful to you, but, after what you have given me to understand, I feel that I must leave you at once. I could never accede to your wishes or assist your plans, and it would be mere presumption in me to inflict on you my true feelings regarding them, or to conjure you to abandon them for better things.'

There was a winning, pleading tone in the last words which banished the distant stateliness of the beginning of this speech, and which should have been touching, vouchsafed by this manly, stalwart fellow of six foot high. But the count, who had looked a little vexed and nettled at first (most probably at his own precipitancy), smoothed his brow and laughed merrily.

'Oh, you English! *toujours au grand sérieux;* when I tell you that there is nothing in my method to which your fastidious honour can object; when I repudiate all designs on you save that of securing your society, for a few weeks at any rate, surely you will return to good humour, surely you will repent of that barbarous idea, nor leave me to the company of that walking brandy-bottle, that still for converting our honest aquavit into curses and ill-humour.'

The friendless man found it hard to

repulse this indomitable cheeriness, to put
from him the sole hand outstretched in this
foreign land to help the penniless refugee
salved from ocean. But he had known ere
now what it was to endure hardness. From
more than one ordeal he had come forth
with his English honour unsullied as his
sole possession, nor was he now for one
moment about to risk its tarnishing. To all
Bjornsen's cajoleries, entreaties, representa-
tions of the impossibility of present escape,
he returned a steady, sorrowful repetition
of his former announcement, 'I must go,
and go at once.' At last the count, invoking
curses in his native tongue on his own folly
in being premature, broke out suddenly,

'Well, then, if nothing else will detain
you even one night under a sinner's polluted

roof, or cheat you of the pleasure of slumbering on our " fjeld " with the wind for a curtain, perhaps family feeling, respect for the chief of your clan, may alter your decision. Know then that Adolphus West, Esquire, of Swardham Hall in Longshire, is even now (in all probability) making such speed from Bergen hither as our roads and our carrioles and the darkness will permit. Remain then, if it is but to greet your relative. Heaven knows, he may well want a sturdy kinsman to back him up in the interview with FitzRaymond, for which he comes. With him, if you still insist, you can travel to Bergen to-morrow or next day. Meanwhile, my silence on certain points shall respect your scruples.'

CHAPTER II.

AQUAVIT.

L EFT to himself the whole of this bright autumnal day, Aylmer FitzRaymond had experienced a change of mood, increasing to ferocity the irritation and restlessness of the morning. It was well for the red-bodiced damsel, well for the sturdy fisherman patching a sail hard by, that they understood none of the mutterings and incoherent exclamations of the stranger, who roamed in and out of the green hostelry aimlessly and incessantly. The day had begun for him with a dawn of

hope—only the sordid hope of enriching
himself in a way from which a man should
have shrunk ; but hope of any description
had not visited this brutalized heart for
many weeks. He had at first sight conceived the profoundest distaste for this
desert solitude to which his friend had
betrayed him. He was without means of
subsistence elsewhere, but he thought that
a winter in Norway, even in Norwegian
towns, would kill him. Turkey and Turkish
ways he had come to like, but this horrible
region, he could not away with it. Then
had come to him amid the first chill of his
disgust an astonishing letter, signed with
a familiar name—a letter dated Bergen,
September 15th, only three days previous !

If he might put faith in this letter, the

present owner of the Swardham estate, of that rental which he had estimated so liberally, was ready to pay down a thousand pounds sterling, and to settle on him an allowance or annuity to boot, on condition that he would part with perhaps the most valueless, the oftenest forgotten possession which remained to him. Georgie,' his pretty cousin, coveted for a while, possessed, abandoned, all but utterly forgotten. And now this wife whom he never meant to see again had a rich fellow anxious to marry her !—lucky for Georgie, she must be *passée*, and would never have sixpence. Why, *any one* should have been welcome to his rights on any terms if a way of selling them were made clear. But after all it would be a trouble—legal formalities were always a trouble—and perhaps a risk, if his hiding-place should be published in English newspapers! With money in his purse, though, he could quickly find fresh hiding-places. What could be better for a man with £1000 than America?—and he felt sure that some device—a commission to take his evidence or what not—could be contrived to spare him the dangers of appearance in a court of justice. He had not forgotten his fright at Liverpool, when he had peered through a port-hole at that miserable cad with whom Eric parleyed so readily, a bailiff no doubt, or a detective, who had tried to board them. How strange that the unlikely story of this other West, this big puritanical lubber with whom Eric seemed unaccountably taken, should be thus quickly and startlingly confirmed! It was well that he had been ousted by a cousin whose blood must be hotter and his notions less scrupulous.

With many such communings the man whiled hours away, roaring now and then to the tidy waitress for more brandy. The girl could not but understand his gestures as he shook the empty flask at her; but to his disgust the liquor with which she presently supplied him was a coarse and inferior spirit. He gulped it down, however, neat, and after many drams began to wax less sanguine, more suspicious. The days were long past when drink made Aylmer FitzRaymond merry or maudlin—a ferocious misanthropy was now the sure result of deep potations, in which he became a

dangerous man, bad to cross, totally irrational. What if this letter were, after
all, a snare, some plant? He believed that
there were those in England and elsewhere
who would be capable of any guile to
entrap him, to bring him to justice, and
perhaps force him to end his days in a
convict's cell.

Hardened and seared as was his conscience, insensible to remorse or shame, he
had still a memory charged with much
guilt, and the terrors of lingering retribu-
tion often gathered thick around him, bath-
ing his temples with sweat, causing his
knees to knock together. It was not of
his mother's broken heart, of his father's
disgraced and ruined old age, that he
thought at such times. He had trans-

gressed the laws. In his desperate need to fill his purse for flight he had outwitted the usurers by dangerous means, and he dreaded vengeance more practical than waits on the curses of a father or a mother's agony.

As darkness came on his mood also darkened, and he had worked himself into distrust and hatred of all things and all men. There was no security in any land, not even in this forsaken spot, for such as he! Even now Bjornsen might be betraying him into the hands of justice, Bjornsen, who always evaded the consequences of his own misdeeds, and was now consorting gaily with this cold, correct Englishman, of whom, pauper and outcast as he deemed him, Aylmer was secretly afraid. Into his heated brain there flashed the mad suspicion that

D 2

there was a conspiracy against him—that those who had sent the letter, and were even now perhaps close at hand, were leagued with his false friend. Scowling around him, he walked stealthily to the door. The girl, who had just brought in a lighted lamp, was now chatting with the boatmen at the door of one of the cottages. It was a peaceful scene enough : dark clouds were gathering overhead, but there was no wind as yet to ripple the waters of the fiord, where the yacht's light showed motionless in the gloom.

But the quietude spoke no comfort to the brandy-soddened wretch ; he closed the door, and locked it ; next he shuttered each window of the room, latching a bar across the solid slabs of deal

seldom used except in the dead of winter;
then, making a round of the ground-floor
apartments, he repeated in each his precautions. The last room visited was the
bar, and here his eyes glared wolfishly at
sight of the kegs and bottles. Snatching
several of the latter, and bearing the lamp
cautiously, he mounted the stair and installed himself in a small room, whose
balconied casement commanded the head
of the fiord, and the rude track by which
he had learned that travellers must approach from Bergen. Meanwhile the count
and John West had parted—for the night
as the former prophesied, for ever according
to the purpose of the latter. When the
pair reached the water's edge a boat was
waiting at a rude landing-place.

'Now think better of it,' Bjornsen said, with one foot in the boat; 'you shall have FitzRaymond's berth, which is fairly comfortable. Let us have a last night on board the old Thyra, which saved you from the fishes. To-morrow or next day she must go round to Bergen, where I hired her eighteen months ago.'

'Where is FitzRaymond then?' Jack queried, without the least intention of availing himself of this offer.

The count motioned toward the fantastic inn.

'Yonder he is, sublimely drunk by this time, I dare say.'

'You don't mean to say that he has the run of that place? Knowing his propensity, you do wrong to allow it.'

'I am tired of keeping him from it. All
I could do was to forbid his being served
with more than one bottle of the more
seductive stuff—even *he* can't swill much
of the vile spirit these people extract from
rye, potatoes—what not? Now are you
coming? No? then good night.'

'Good-bye,' Jack answered, and turned
sadly away.

There was so much in this man that was
fascinating that he grieved to be running
away, as it were, thanklessly from his
hospitality. But in these days of his abased
state he was more than ever sensitive where
his honour might be compromised—it was
all that remained to him. He must quit
the company of a self-confessed gambler
with all speed, it was his duty to himself.

With another duty his mind was also charged. He must go to the British consul at Bergen and take measures for the enlightenment of Hilda Fife's friends as to her fate—too long left undisclosed by the sole witness of it. The night had become so dark, neither star nor moon being visible, that during the short walk from the landing-place to the inn (where a light shone in an upper chamber) Jack had convinced himself that it would be useless to attempt a lonely walk over an unknown country. He would lie down in the room where they had eaten, and start before any one should be stirring, with the first gleam of dawn. Feeling his way to the porch, he tried to enter gently, but the door would not yield. He shook it once or twice, and then turned

to look at the neighbouring huts. All was
dark and still. Plainly the peasants were
in the habit of going early to bed. Then
he went round the wooden building with
its many angles and quaint roofs, till he
stood beneath the window where the light
was. Here at least some one was stirring.
He could hear shuffling feet upon the little
balcony. Stepping a little back, he looked
up and essayed his sole Norse sentence, a
conciliatory '*Ver sa gud*—' but stopped
short as a head leaned over the fanciful
balustrade. No features were discernible,
but, outlined against the lighted window,
the head looked unpleasant enough, with
wild hair fringing it in spiky disorder.
For a moment there was silence, then a
voice, huskily malignant, yelled out curses

and threats in an ugly mixture of many tongues, among which English was dominant. So hideous was the discord of blasphemy and menace that the listener recoiled into the darkness, failing at once to recognize FitzRaymond's voice.

As he walked slowly away, however, along the rough road leading inland, Jack was filled with wrath against his late host. Why had he brought this miserable man here to abandon him to his madness? Much as he loathed Aylmer, he thought that he must endeavour in some way, by invoking some gracious Englishman, if such he could find, to rescue the man from this place and plight, and afford him such surveillance as he needed till his relations could be communicated with. For himself, he did not much dread a night in the open, though the country was Norway and the month late autumn. He would go slowly on till he was quite tired, and then a short sleep might be possible under the lee of a rock, or, if he were lucky, in some shed. His thoughts turned ever on Bjornsen. What horror he had expressed, this man who lived on the follies of his fellows, at the prospect of one gently-nurtured stooping to labour with his hands for daily bread! It reminded him of the misguided Hilda Fife, with her taunts as to 'soulless hinds,' and her insane offers of release from their lot. He could scarcely decide which would have been more impossible to him—to sell himself in wedlock with a woman he disliked, or to cast in his lot with a gambler, wandering from one resort to another of knaves and their dupes! Was there anything in him, he wondered, which should peculiarly provoke such base proposals, or was it always the bitterest drop in the cup of such as he, that the stamp of gentle blood and rearing should be ineffaceable, and should forbid belief that a penniless gentleman could possess a sense of honour or be self-respecting amid his destitution?

Pondering gloomily, he made way more expeditiously than he had expected: already he had climbed a ridge, and left the fiord behind, descending into a long valley, where the road was somewhat better. At last he saw far ahead two moving points of light, small and dim, slowly descending, as it seemed, a steep hill and advancing towards him. Encouraged by the prospect of encountering wayfarers who might direct him, he walked briskly on, ever nearing the lights. While yet some distance intervened, he could hear a voice, and soon discovered with surprise that fretful exclamations were being uttered in his own language.

In another minute he could make out that two men bearing lanterns were approaching him on foot—of whom the foremost was silent, while the other was groaning over the roughness of the way, and complaining that his attendant did not assist him by holding his lantern low enough. Surely he had heard that voice in the past, or why did it stir his breast painfully? It was the voice, yes, and the figure of his cousin! Once more had fate brought about an

unwelcome meeting with this man, whose
star was so adverse to his own.

Benighted and ill-at-ease, Adolphus was,
as Bjornsen had told him, making his way
to a meeting with the raving maniac,
Aylmer FitzRaymond. As he stood stock
still in the middle of the road, the man
who walked in front flashed his lantern full
upon his face, and in an instant his cousin
too had recognized the handsome features,
the towering head, which had confronted
him, once in Hockerill's barn, and a second
and last time (as both imagined) in Scott's
office at Longborough; had noted the broad
chest and stalwart arms which had once
seized on him as a hawk might seize a
chicken. The suspense, worry, and fatigue
of his life since he had left Swardham

without companion or adviser, and not least certain untoward events of the evening, had considerably unhinged Adolphus West, whose temper, never of the best, was just now at a gusty pitch. He had reached Bergen, safe but prostrate with sea-sickness, before the Thyra, an old boat, under-manned and badly engined, had so much as rounded Duncansby Head. Then had begun a second spell of feverish waiting such as he had endured at Liverpool. For the beauties of Bergen, a really pretty place if the weather is fine, or the study of Norse manners and customs, he had not the most transient relish, his every faculty being engrossed in his mission, and in longings to return to her for whose sake it was undertaken. He had been introduced by the keeper of his hotel to a polite merchant, who spoke excellent English, and was acquainted with Count Bjornsen, being indeed the owner and lessor of the **Thyra.** This gentleman in vain exhorted West to take things easily, as the yacht was doubtless doing, and to trust him to supply instant information of her arrival. So long did the delay seem to Adolphus that he began to half hope half fear that the vessel might have gone to the bottom. It would be excellent that Lady G. should thus become a widow, but then it might be difficult to prove that her husband had perished on the main. At last a revenue cutter came in which had spoken and boarded the Thyra only a few hours previous, and brought a message to her owner, and a request that letters might be forwarded from the Bergen post-office to Bjornestrand. It was with difficulty that Adolphus was persuaded by his friend to despatch a letter, instead of starting at once in person for the count's abode. But for the remembrance indeed of his ill-success at Liverpool he could not have been restrained an hour.

At last, however, he set off, having allowed bare time for Aylmer FitzRaymond to land and receive the letter. The sight of a carriole filled him with huge indignation; he was for sending away the 'big wooden shoe on shafts and wheels,' and ordering round a brougham, till assured that Bergen knew no broughams, and that to Bjornestrand, at any rate, no other class of vehicle could possibly make its way. In a carriole therefore, ill-contented, he started betimes, following another carriole of somewhat less slipper-like dimensions, which bore his valise and a Norseman who spoke a little English, and was to act as guide. For the very timid or the very luxurious a carriole journey of twenty-five miles over byroads in Norway is not to be recommended. Now Adolphus was constitutionally timid, and in these later days more prone to resent discomfort than many another to whom discomfort had never been of daily occurrence. The Norwegian ponies are marvels. Let them alone, and they never stumble or do wrong, not in descending the most awful hill, where the tenant of the greatly sloping carriole loses sight of all but the cream-coloured tail, and perchance

the ear-tips of his steed. But Adolphus
would not believe in the virtues of the
ponies; he would give frantic tugs at his
reins, which the innocent beast was obliged
to resent; and far from becoming convinced
of his error as the day wore on, he comported
himself more and more outrageously at each
hill he descended, and suffered therefore
many things, including bruises and woeful
loss of time. Thus it betided that night
had fallen darkly when the carrioles arrived
at the brink of a sort of precipice, from
which the soul of Adolphus recoiled in
horror.

'Bjornestrand,' said the much-enduring
guide in a mild and cheerful tone, and
pointed as he spoke to a distant speck or
two of light—far, far below.

But the cheerfulness vanished when the Norseman was made to understand that his convoy absolutely refused to proceed 'down a place like the roof of a house, in pitchy darkness.' To Bjornestrand by all means, but on foot! Deaf to all the guide's expostulations and growls, Adolphus insisted on his leaving the horses and carrioles (which he would scarcely allow the man to secure in a little copse of birch), and preceding him, valise on back and lantern in hand. Slowly and painfully, with many an unpleasant trip and wrench among the stones, and many an execration, the owner of Swardham hobbled on, thinking incessantly of the pending interview, and the triumph to come of it. There would be no attempt to evade him on *this* occasion ; no misinterpretation

of his design ; he carried the golden key
which was to ensure respect and compliance.
The five thousand was banked at Bergen,
and he was prepared to be lavish in clearing away all hindrances to his speedy
marriage with Georgiana. But for this—
and this was only a joy in prospect, as
yet untasted—how little pleasure or satisfaction had the revenues of that Swardham
estate brought him whom man deemed so
marvellously fortunate! But for this—and
what present torment he had had in com-
passing this, this mere step to future bliss!

And did bliss really await him, when the
last obstacle should be swept away, and
that beautiful hand should indeed be his?
Ah! he refused, in a frenzy, to weigh probabilities. She would be his—that was

enough.   She, the most enchanting of all beauties, his wife, his own ! without whom house, lands, money were all worthless— might as well still belong to that old haughty image who was wandered away in poverty, none knew where.

At this very instant, as if invoked by his passing thought, his cousin's form appeared from out the deepening darkness—appeared close at hand, with lips parted as if to speak, and hands outstretched as if to bar the way—appeared as though dropped from the skies in this remote and desolate spot to thwart his kinsman's purpose.   There still rankled in the heart of Adolphus West hatred against this man who had not whined or cringed, nor in any way lost his dignity under the most trying of reverses.

Even at this moment it flashed upon his memory how, at that last interview, his cousin had commended the Swardham tenantry to his tenderest mercies. He had resented such recommendation, and still resented it, with Clarke's letter in his pocket telling him of the last audit, at which most of the farmers, pleading the failure of their crops, had begged hard and humbly for an abatement of the full rent due.

Clarke's letter had been answered yesterday, thus— 'I expect every penny that is owing to me ; put on the screw if you can't get it without.' Thus it was that John West's apparition looked to him reproachful, and he hated him for that fancied reproach and for his inopportune presence. How true is Thackeray's observation that there is no character which a low-minded man so much mistrusts as that of a gentleman. And it is usually aggressive mistrust. The secret terror of a ' better gentleman ' breeds oftener irritation than awe in the bosom, at any rate, of the low-minded who has the pull over his superior in the accidents of wealth.

Knitting his pale brows, the rich man was for passing on with no more than a nod, but the poor relation stretched a strong arm across his path and began earnestly,

' Cousin Adolphus, perhaps you hardly know me, meeting me here so unexpectedly ; but I knew of your being in Norway, and have just come from the place you are going toward. And I trust you won't set me down for a meddler if I beg you not to think of seeing Aylmer FitzRaymond to-night. Whatever your business with him may be, he is in no condition to hear it. Indeed, I fear that even to-morrow he will scarcely be fit; but to-night he is more than unfit—he is positively savage.'

Adolphus snorted with displeasure, and answered in would-be lofty style,—

'Perhaps the savagery of which you speak may have been due to some such obtrusion of unsolicited advice or company as you are now favouring me with. In any case, sir, my errand with this gentleman, however you come to know it so accurately, is one that won't admit of delay, and I wish you good night, sir, and business of your own to mind.'

With these rude words of anti-climax he

was passing on, his puny figure drawn up
to its highest, when once more his cousin
sought to detain him.

'I beg you, go at least to one of the
cottages at Bjornestrand, not to the inn ;
you can stop the night in one of the huts.
The man is downright raving, I tell you
— mad with drink.'

He laid his hand on the other's shoulder
as he spoke and kept it there, by a slight
pressure, when Adolphus wriggled and strove
to shake it off. But when he had finished
his sentence he plucked away his hand
with a mighty impulse, to bring it crashing
down in all its might on his cousin's pale
red head. Adolphus, acting as a spoiled
boy might in the clutch of a nurse-maid,
had rapped him smartly over the fingers

with the silver knob of his walking-stick. It was a mere nothing, viewed as an assault, but for a second it was like to have let loose on the striker such a battery as would have marked him for life.

But the second of roused ferocity was over; Adolphus was walking on, at a brisk pace, toward Bjornestrand, and John was standing still in the middle of the road, gulping down the subsiding emotions (of which he was ashamed already) and rubbing his knuckles.

'Well,' he said aloud, presently, 'I am getting on. Not that it's much credit to refrain from hitting back such a weed as he is—the chief of my clan, forsooth! with whom I was to journey so agreeably to

Bergen to-morrow. They say that "naught is never in danger," and on that principle Adolphus should come off unscathed; but if he really beards FitzRaymond to-night he will certainly be frightened if not hurt. Perhaps he will pay more attention to my warning after all, though, than he gave me to understand by his behaviour.'

He had begun to trudge forward again, and for a time plodded on, climbing with difficulty the steep hill on which he had first spied the lanterns. Suddenly he stopped.

'What a mean beast I am, after all,' he broke out, 'to take credit to myself for not hitting that little chap, and let him walk off into the jaws of—God knows what! After all, blood is thicker than water, he is my mother's brother's son; and what have the Wests come to if one lets another run a risk alone in this fashion? I will just toddle back, and if all goes quietly, no one need be the wiser for my presence. I'll be off again early. But if there is a row I'll stand by the head of the family, ill-conditioned weakling as he is, which gives all the more reason for my loyalty, by-the-bye.'

And whistling a blithe tune, John West strode down the hill, with his face set once more for Bjornestrand.

CHAPTER III.

THE GOOD SERVANT THAT IS A BAD MASTER.

RUFFLED by his encounter with his cousin, Adolphus West was so abominably testy with his unfortunate guide, that the latter had no sooner let fall the valise with a flop on the doorstep of Count Bjornsen's green pagoda (where a light still shone in an upper window), than he walked doggedly off without a word, regardless of his employer's shouts, and was soon lost in the darkness. He had his horses and carrioles to look after, and he yearned for the society of the dumb brutes by way of a change. He knew every inch of the ground, and struck into a narrow path, which would take him by a shorter but steeper route to the spot where the animals were tethered. Perhaps by next morning he should find the Englishman in a better temper. Meanwhile, he knew of a hay-barn where to lodge for the night; and preferred supping on a crust in his pocket to his chance of sharing even a stalled ox in contentious company.

Left to himself, the exasperated Adolphus began to thump loudly at the nearest door, shouting for admittance. He did not believe the account of Aylmer FitzRaymond's state : it was an invention of that evil one. Supposing the man should be rather drunk —he had seen plenty of drunken men. He

had seen Jemmy Clancy very drunk indeed,
and knew that at such times he would be
tearful and ready to promise anything.
To-morrow the odious cousin might return
(he said he had been at this place) and
thrust in his interfering oar where it was
not wanted. Perhaps he thought it his
interest to keep him, Adolphus, from marry-
ing, in the hope of outliving him and
inheriting Swardham again ; whereas—' Ah-
ha !' Just then a window was opened, and
a drowsy, surly voice, an English voice,
demanded gruffly who was there ? West's
heart throbbed high ; he felt sure that he
heard the man whom he had sought from
east to west of Europe, the man who was
the present bar to his felicity.

'I am here to see Colonel FitzRaymond,'

he called out in his best tone, 'on important business much to his advantage, as set forth in my letter. I am Mr. West of Swardham.'

There was a pause; some one leaned over a balcony and asked suspiciously,

'How many of you are there?'

'I am alone,' said Adolphus, gaining confidence; 'the brute of a guide has gone off. If you'll just let me in, I'm sure we can settle our affairs most amicably, all the better for no one else being by.'

'You're sure there are no fellows hiding anywhere round the house?' the voice replied; and Adolphus protested vigorously that there was no one.

Then he heard shuffling steps descend a stair, and the door was unlocked, and a head cautiously protruded from the blacker darkness within.

'I'm the man you want then, Mr. West; and you may come up,' was whispered hoarsely.

And Adolphus, stepping inside, was bidden to mount the stair towards a glimmer of light, while the other locked the door again, taking a long while about the operation.

The drunkard had fallen into a sleep after his outburst of violence towards John West, and was now in a half-stupid state, in which his maniac ferocity smouldered obscurely, latent for the moment, while his mind dimly resumed the more hopeful attitude of the morning. Stopping on the stairs, he fumbled at his pocket, and found a bottle half full of the vile brandy which he had appropriated from the bar. Of this he took a long draught, by way of clearing his faculties for business, and then followed his visitor into the room. Standing in the door-way to reconnoitre, he saw a slight figure stooping over the table, which, with the oil-lamp burning brightly upon it, stood between the two men. The stranger was pulling papers from his pockets, and laying them upon the table, and from his posture FitzRaymond could see little of his appearance except a shock head of pale red hair. But in another instant the stooping figure stood upright and faced him, and in that same instant revealed the well-remembered features of the 'cad,' the spy, bailiff, or detective who had tried to board the Thyra in the Mersey.

And did this hound think to pass for West of Swardham? Death to him! vengeance on the conspirator! Uttering a horrible yell, and staggering with the drunken fury that leapt up in him like a slumbering tiger aroused, Aylmer FitzRaymond whirled the bottle round his head and flung it at that hateful face. But his aim was marred by his very rage; the bottle missed its mark, and struck the lamp, which was broken and hurled in fragments from the table. For a moment there was partial darkness in the room, but then, as the madman uttered another yell and prepared to rush upon his affrighted and cowering victim, a barrier of fire arose between them.

The coarse mineral oil, flowing over the boards and mixing with the spirit from the

shattered bottle, flashed into a sheet of flame,
which sprang at once upon the dry wood-
work, and made even FitzRaymond recoil
aghast.   The table, the papers, the flooring
around were burning fiercely in a single
second.   In another the partition was licked
by tongues of fire, and yielded its seasoned
planks of pine a ready prey.

Crazy with terror, Adolphus tore open the
window, and hanging over the railing of the
little balcony, shrieked aloud for help.   He
was minded to drop himself to the ground,
and actually clambered the railing and hung,
for an instant, by his hands, with dangled
legs.   But the unknown depth of the fall,
all veiled in darkness, appalled him.   He
drew himself, with shaking arms, back into
the balcony, scarce knowing whether he

dreaded more the flames or the terrible haggard figure who had striven to brain him. Of the latter nothing was to be seen just now. He had heard him laugh a demoniac yell of laughter; but he had disappeared, and the room was tenanted only by the flickering leaping flames, which seemed to bar the way. The draught from the open window, the door of the room being also open, had assisted the spread of the fire, which, as it gained strength, lifted up its voice in a sustained and awful roaring. Smoke also, the pungent smoke of burning fir-wood, began to roll through the casement in volumes, stopping the breath and blinding the eyes, and the heat smote painfully on face and hands.

Redoubling his screams, Adolphus pushed

to the window behind him, and shut himself out on the tiny balcony, a mere ledge of less than two feet in width. He felt now that he would gladly face the most furious human violence, if he might only be delivered from this more ruthless destroyer, whose breath was already encompassing him. Why had he not made a dash for the door ere yet the pool of burning oil had soaked the flooring? Better have died in the clutch of that murderous wretch than perish by fire. Would no one come to help? Was this horrible place deserted of all save one furious madman? He thought of John West's advice, and gnashed his teeth. Hoarse with his cries, he continued to strain his throat, while his flesh crept with horror. The glass of the window cracked with the increasing heat within, and falling outward in pieces, let a hellish blast upon him as of scorching wind. Voices at last below! voices and hurrying steps!

'Help!' he cried; 'I am here! help, or I shall be burned! I am West of Swardham! Squire West! A hundred pounds! five hundred! a thousand! to any one who will fetch a ladder and get me down safe.'

Frantically he repeated his offers. Oh God! they did not understand a word he said, these miserable peasants. Where was that cruel guide, who might have told them? Surely there must be a way even if they had no ladder—a way that money could find, if they could only be made to understand how much money he would give?

But among the little group of bewildered,

half-sleepy people who had rushed from
the huts, wrapped in quilts and garments
hastily snatched, there was now one who
did hear and understand—a tall man
panting with the speed at which he had
hastened to the spot on hearing distant
shrieks, and seeing a strange light which
low heavy clouds were reflecting strangely.
As John West appeared on the scene his
unhappy cousin was making a last appeal
to the few stolid folk who stood and stared
like oxen. The more stirring spirits among
them had manned a boat and rowed off to
rouse the count, snug in his berth a quarter
of a mile away. Those remaining were
disabled by apathy or a sort of paralysis,
only holding up their hands and shaking
their heads when the figure at the window

vanished with a last howl of despair, as denser smoke and flame poured through the opening.

Perceiving that nothing was to be hoped from the co-operation of the bystanders, John West rapidly eyed the building, with its locked doors and shuttered lower windows. The upper casements were all lit up now by the red glow within, and a wind rising from the sea was driving thick smoke before it and fanning the blaze. He must break his way in! The trunk of a fir lay near—and when they saw him trying to handle it, two lads came to his assistance, and helped to wield it as a battering-ram against the door of the bar-room. The hinges gave way at last, and the door was thrust inwards. Already was fire dropping through the wooden ceiling, dropping on those rows of kegs and barrels; no time was to be lost. The lads recoiled before the smoke and heat, but John West ran through the room to the foot of the staircase, and tried to mount. He held his breath, he crouched as he ascended, but every upward step was more terrible. The heat, the smoke redoubled, and he turned and rushed once more to the outer air, not, however, to abandon his efforts. Without a word, he seized on a small sail which lay across a bench, and dipped it in the cold water of the fiord. Then flinging it round his shoulders, he re-entered the doomed house.

Oh, heaven! how terrible was the heat, blistering even the lower steps of that stairway; how the fire roared and crackled

overhead! Muttering a prayer, he wrapped
the wet canvas round head and shoulders,
holding a corner between his strong white
teeth. On hands and knees he climbed the
stair, confused and agonized by the hideous
turmoil, but, thank God! enabled by his
rude respirator to get his breath and to
ascend!

As his hands shrank from the wood that
scorched them, he clutched the sail tight,
bunching it under his palms, and peered
through the doorway, which he had at
last reached. His hair and eyebrows were
instantly scorched and frizzled : the place
within was a hell of flames which none
might penetrate and live. Must he retreat
once more, leaving his kinsman to this
horrid fate? He thrust at the half-open

door; ah! there was something behind it—
something lying on the blistering planks
with flames already lapping it.   Holding
his breath, he reached round the door and
clutched the object: it was the body of a
man, lifeless and limp, an unresisting prey
to the greedy blaze.   In another instant,
which seemed long from the frightful
exposure to furnace heat and darting
tongues of fire, he had grasped the figure
and dragged it round the door—wrapping
it, hugged by one arm to his own breast,
beneath the folds of the sail.   Then, headlong, almost swooning, but still crouching
close to the flooring, he launched himself
and his burden down the steep stair.
Desperately he crawled with his heavy
burden, bruised and burned, but still holding

tight. The bar-room was now alight, flakes of fire raining into it through the rafters above; and as he crept through it, often setting bare hands and bleeding knees on hot embers, he had the horrible dread upon him that he might be overwhelmed by some vast mass of glowing wreck, some heavy beam, or net-work of joists. Or what if he were to miss the door? His strength was nearly spent. He was dazed and anguished, and seemed to be swallowing the breath of a furnace. Another minute must be decisive. The sill at last! a whiff of cooler air! A last frantic drag, and his hands touched the cool gravel. It was over! He was safe, still grasping his burden, from whom the old sail dropped, all smouldering and smoking. Then he felt himself seized and pulled further into the air, the delicious, life-restoring air.   But the raw agony of his burns, handled by the rude strength of his succourers, was too much for him.   He fainted before he could look upon the unconscious form of him whom he had rescued.

Meanwhile the fire was asserting itself more and more imperious and irresistible. No longer content with devouring the entrails of the house, and looking from its windows in red streamers or jets of stifling smoke, it was soaring now in one strong column from a great gap where a roof had collapsed and gables fallen inwards.   The low black clouds, from which a few heavy drops began to fall, felt its influence, and flushed angrily before they could escape the crimsoned circle which hung like an unholy aureole over its jagged head. The central turret of the edifice was not yet ablaze, but its fate was plain. Though the rising breeze swayed away from it the surging flames that far out-topped it, its supports were on one side sapped and gone. Already its dark outline was all aslant; in a few minutes it must topple into that gap towards which it leaned—the gap whence rose triumphant that awful pillar of fire.

The bystanders watched, powerless and dumb, till this plunge should take effect; they could see the flag-staff rock, it must soon go down. But it was fated that a more thrilling, a more horrible interest should attach to this short watch. Suddenly a dark shape was seen to emerge from the turret's top, and fling an arm around the flag-staff. Above the importunate clamour of the conflagration could be heard defiant yells, scarcely human in sound, and as his perch nodded to its fall, a man was seen to shake his clenched fist downwards, and wave his arm wildly. It was a sight which none who saw it could forget, a horrible moment of hopeless suspense. As the structure gave its final lurch, the wretch seemed to loose his hold, and to dive headlong into the chasm of fire. For a moment the upward current of flame was checked, as the turret was hurled upon it, but the next moment it soared higher than ever, as if rejoicing to find amid its new fuel a human being—to have its will of one of the race who have made it their slave and drudge.

Out of the gulf into which Aylmer Fitz-Raymond went down a living man not a trace of him, not so much as a charred bone, was ever retrieved. 'His veins ran brandy rather than blood,' said one of the fisher people to another three days afterwards, who vainly searched amid the ashes. These were caked by incessant rains, which, beginning the very night of the fire, lasted for weeks without intermission. Vainly did they sift with sieves the clotted dust, and thrust aside with spades the crumbling ruin.

'Yes, brandy, not blood. We shall no more find him than we shall find a stave of the kegs that stood in the bar.'

This was Aylmer's epitaph. Of all mankind there was not one to honour him with better, to mourn his loss or cherish his memory, to 'lament for him saying, Ah, my brother, or Ah, his glory.'   From that early day, when the well-born, handsome boy was gazetted, to the last, when the haggard and disgraced man had scowled, with dark presentiment, upon the spot of earth where his frame should be that night annihilated, he had never fulfilled one duty honestly, or done one deed of love or charity, or struggled against a vice; rather had he never ceased to abuse his powers and opportunities, and to squander in selfish devilry the gifts which had been his.   And now, without one moment for a remorseful thought, or a prayer of penitence, with all his sins upon his head, he was gone to his own place, earth retaining of him not so much as the buried bones.

CHAPTER IV.

PATIENT GRISELDA.

'DO you know, Mary, that you have become ever so disagreeable lately?'

It was Miss Holbrooke's friend and neighbour, Fanny Morgan, who tried to frown as she thus impeached her friend in the rectory drawing-room, and shook a little tea-spoon at her. 'Yes, it's all very well to raise your eyebrows: you have the advantage of me there, because mine are invisible white, and it's not a bit of use my arching them; but the fact remains.

You are not cross or in any way absolutely horrid, because you couldn't be if you tried; but you have left off caring about everything that you especially ought to find interesting—there ! '

Mary hastened to assure her friend that she had not left off caring for *her*, which brought on her a hug from the plump and rosy Fanny, who, however, ran on—

' No ; one can't pick a hole in you or a quarrel with you, you are quite provokingly good ; but you were always as good as anybody need be in the days when you had plenty of fun in you too, and cared a bit, like the rest of us, about dressing and going out, and so on. Now, look here, Mary ; a really good girl does far more with her goodness when she is like what

you were than if she turns extra-super, and
can't care for such trivialities as enchant
poor me.   So you see, as a matter of
influence and example, and all that, it's
quite a mistake, if not wicked, to forsake
the ways of your guileless youth for a
severer style.'

'Why, Fanny, I don't know myself in
this new character of mine.   Among the
" unco guid " I never thought to rank ; and
as to holding myself *above* anybody or anything familiar to me, if that is what extra-
super means, such a notion never occurred
to me.   But one can't always be quite
merry and easy ; I wish we could.   I think
no one in Swardham parish *can* carry
the light heart of the old time, least of all
poor dear papa.   And when *he* is sad,

Fanny, his only child must be saddened too.'

Fanny shook her head.

'My dear,' she said, 'life is not *all* parochial, even for the parson and his family; the more there is in the parish to distress your father and you (and I'm not denying that all the changes seem greatly for the worse), the more thankful you both ought to be for a little enlivenment outside the parish. Now, your father goes, at any rate, to the rural dean's, and the clerical book-club meetings, and dinners, and all that, and you ought to go to anything social that is in *your* line, whereas—Oh! Mary, you that did so love a dance; you shirked the Barbers, the jolliest hop this year, and as you couldn't utterly shirk our little affair, sat and played the piano after the first two squares like the veriest old auntie, and decamped at eleven. Oh! Mary, and you think you are not disagreeable!'

Mary laughed at this enumeration of her crimes; Fanny looked so like the portly rector her father as she shook her fat cheeks, that she could not help laughing: and for the remainder of the visit strove to be as gay as her friend would have her. But in so doing she was conscious of effort.

Alas! all her life had been an effort, a struggle to play a part that was growing more hard and spiritless every day since the morning on which John West had stolen away from the rectory, leaving nothing behind him save that short note of farewell. She might never tell any one, not even her father, of the passage between them, that strange short spell of bliss, which had vanished and left no trace save in the recesses of a girl's heart. Mary was patient and uncomplaining even in communing with her own sad spirit.

Many would blame the girl for tameness. 'Continue to care for a man who told his love one day and bólted the next! She is too lacking in spirit and proper pride to deserve better luck.' In truth, this is no age for patient Griselda. If such a character be found, not admiration, but scoffs and sneers are heaped upon it by female critics. Mary's attitude of mind and spirit before her love was full as lowly as Griselda's before her perverse-seeming lord.

She would have cared nothing for the verdict of nineteenth century maidenhood had her fond clinging to that fugitive love's memory been as public as it was the reverse. She knew his nature so well. Had she not all her days been studying him, and that dear mother whom he so much resembled? He could not equally have sounded the depths of her own soul. But the other day she had been to him an insignificant child, a plaything at best; and though one marvellous moment had revealed her tender worship to him in such fashion that he had taken her into his heart of hearts, it was not strange that he should deem it possible for one so recently emerged from girlhood to listen to another lover. Children are so.

Time was when a youth, comely and
gentle, wealthy, and favoured by her father's
approbation, might have set Mary's heart
in a quick flutter, which might as quickly
have passed. But she was a woman now,
and she loved, once and for all. She could
wait, suffer, do anything but change; so
she did not call her lover cruel, far less
false. She knew that his words had come
from the heart, that his kisses (she could
count those kisses) had been pledges of
love unfeigned and most honourable. It
was that honour, she readily believed, which
in its sensitiveness had urged him to crush
down his love just as it sprang up fair
and fresh; but oh, the pity of it! Why
could she not tell him all that was in her
heart? She had never loved but him—

never could love another, be his wooing backed by all the world and its wealth. And it would make no difference if fate refused her all chance of whispering her fidelity into John West's ear. Ah! fate was hard, for it surely would have cheered his lonely life of toil to know his Mary faithful. She could not fear that Mary was forgotten; his was not the nature to be light or fickle. He would leave her, but not cease to cherish her in his true heart. They would go down to their graves, perhaps far, far apart, each loving the other always, but with little hope or none.

And yet she would not have given up her romance, her momentary bliss with its sequel of doubt and separation, for the

brightest lot shared with another.   She
thought, as days followed days and brought
no news, that in heaven she would meet
Rachel West, and hear her whisper, ' We two
loved him best,' and the thought was sweet
to her.

As to young Herbert, his proposed offer
had never been made. The rector was so little
versed in secrecy or manœuvre that the drift
of Mr. Herbert's overture leaked out to his
girl in the course of a single day. She had
been in some measure prepared for such
approach by the short, miserable note which
John West had left for her. Her love made
her quick to divine and understand. Jack's
abrupt departure, her father's pre-occupation
and little cheerful mystery, she soon put
these facts together. The note and the

departure had been an almost crushing disappointment; but Mary was young and elastic, and before she had time to be bent by adversity, before she had been many hours in possession of that sad farewell of her lover, lo! his departure was explained, and hope revived. It was not that he repented of stooping to one so unworthy of him. Surely he would not go away so far that no word could reach him. Surely he would be left in little doubt as to young Herbert's reception by herself, if reception there should ever be.

Greatly was the good rector discomfited at his own want of tact and finesse when his daughter calmly ended his blundering and hinting by 'seeing' (as he said) 'through the whole thing in a trice,' and begging her

father to save her pain by at once informing
Mr. Herbert that his son's suit was im-
practicable. Mary convinced the good man
at last that it was not owing to his
incaution that the intended wooing had
miscarried.

'If young Mr. Herbert, and old Mr.
Herbert too, had come here and stayed
months, it would have made no manner
of difference, papa. And as you would
never do for a conspirator, it is very well
that you are spared the ordeal.'

The rector marvelled, but could not
grumble at his daughter's determination to
remain by him 'for ever and always,' she
said. He had much, as the summer advanced, to occupy him by turning his mind
from his own grievances to those of others.

It was a bad, nay, a disastrous season for many of his most substantial and valued parishioners. The acreage of Swardham parish is pretty equally divided between arable and pasture land. Thus in former years, if a bad harvest had befallen, some compensation still remained to the farmer in his beeves. If, again, prices ruled unprofitably low for stock and cattle, by the help of abundant grain the depreciation would be tided over. Moreover, in the event of losses out-balancing profits, there was always safe recourse to Squire West (no matter which of them it might be), who never turned a deaf ear to a genuine tale of distress, and would often go beyond the petitioner's request in according timely relief. But in the present season the farmers of Swardham were encountering

such adversity as they never knew before.
Their harvest was a failure, owing to a
terribly wet July and August, and alas!
there was not a yard in which murrain had
not attacked their beasts. The animals
unaffected by the pest might not be driven
to market or fair; the very milk and butter
were suspected, and had almost to be
given away, to be re-sold by mere higglers
to the lowest classes in neighbouring
towns.

In their affliction the farmers were mind-
ful of the one resource left to them. They
must invoke the clemency of their landlord.
He was indeed a man of strange and
unfamiliar type; but he *was*, after all,
a genuine-born West, grandson to the old
squire; he could not refuse the prayer of

his tenantry in their direst day of trouble. Many an old-fashioned gig and many a stout cob or sinewy hunter passed up the old elm avenue, bearing their brawny, healthy owners, all bound upon the same errand, to 'have it out' with the squire. Alas! for their sturdy confidence ; the tall windows were shuttered, the chimneys smokeless. A sulky stranger butler, arrayed in the coloured clothes of servant's holiday, scarce opened that side door, hard by the old justice room and steward's room, to which the tenantry had ever repaired on their visits. The chain rattled as the indifferent answer was flung in each weather-beaten face,—

'Master's away, travelling. Back? can't say, I'm shaw.'

There was a speedy clearance; whip and spur plied in that old avenue as never had they been plied by tenants leaving the old home of the Wests. Some old faces looked very pulled and sunken, as their owners drove into the farmyards that day; some younger ones very reckless and desperate. Apply to lawyer Clark! Ah, to be sure, they would apply, and tell a plain tale. But did ever any good come of an application through a lawyer? So little was the hope left to them when the house of the Wests had kept its doors shut on them, that the answer which came in time through the lawyer from the absentee created little sensation. Of course he would have no mercy, this Squire West who left the old Hall to turn chained doors and shuttered windows on

H 2

his own people when they went there in distress.

'Over two hundred year we have bin on this farm, from father to son, under the Wests,' so said old Everett of Danes farm, 'and now we mun go, go and work for wage.'

There was little invective, little outward sign of their woe among the hardest hit of these men; but their rector knew them, knew their very hearts, and his own heart bled for them. Here was indeed a trial for a good man's faith. He taught others, and was bound himself to believe that One above orders all things sublunary for the wisest and most salutary ends; but ah! it was hard to include in that great rule the event which had flung John West on the world and raised Adolphus in his place. And the parson was so powerless, so utterly powerless. Even had the squire chosen to remain in Swardham, and chosen to receive him, he knew that his solicitude would rather prejudice the chances of his clients.

A less sensitive man than Francis Holbrooke would have been well aware that for him Adolphus West had no love. It lay, in fact, at the root of this dislike, that the rector had first seen the new squire amid the squalors of Britannia Street; he was besides a partisan of the old *régime*, and as such to be kept at arm's length.

The poor rector, as was usual with him, blamed himself for not having created a

better impression on the new-comer. There
were gifted men, he thought, who might
have influenced for good a young man
suddenly elevated to such a position, no
matter what his temper or antecedents.
There was an archdeacon, there were one
or two rural deans and rectors of his acquaintance, who might, he thought, have
coped with even Adolphus West, had they
held sway in Swardham parish. Dignified
men, yet strong in argument, suave, yet
very firm, they must at least have quenched
the stubborn rudeness over which he could
but sigh. For, alas! his gifts were of no
such high order : he could scarcely maintain a decent semblance of civility with his
dear Jack West's supplanter, as Jack would
certainly have had him do. True, it would

have been hard to live in amity with so odd a character, but it *might* have been; and, ah! with what possible happy effect for these honest fellows, the pride of the parish and the county, who must now lose their holdings in bankruptcy and be plunged in misery, mainly (so he told himself) because their parish priest was a poor blunderer—one who, spite of his high office and calling, wielded no power for good.

In such strain was the poor rector wont to fret, bemoaning his helplessness, not selfishly, but for the sake of his loved flock. But he wronged himself in imputing incapacity to his ministrations. All that a sympathetic presence could do for the families who were pressed most sorely— counsel, comfort, even cash, though tithes were in sad arrears, were forthcoming from the self-distrusting pastor. It was a labour of love as well as a most sacred duty. Not only did he love his people, but in doing his best for their needs he gave expression to his consecrated affection for Rachel West and her son. God had been pleased to remove from him both. Then to tend their former charges was all he could still do for them. The difficulties of their employers had reacted on the labouring poor of the place, and in many a lowly cottage, where the 'master' was out of work, and the cupboard was empty, did the rector bid hunger avaunt from good wives and children ; for many a stout hind did he obtain a job in some less troubled neigh-bourhood.

It was in such occupations, and the fond talk that would spring up among these poor ones as to happier times, that he now found his most cheerful hours. When he was at home, not even Mary's presence could keep his thoughts from sad roamings through the vanished happiness of the past, or sad excursions into the vague unknown, always in quest of Jack West. What was he doing? Why did he not write again? When, oh, when would his oldest friend be rejoiced once more by sight of that fine lofty brow, that stalwart form, those calm grey eyes? Sometimes he would recall, with a momentary feeling of indignation, that was almost superstitious in origin, the prophecies of that evil stranger, which had been so strangely fulfilled. Alas, for the Arcadia of the past, that pleasant, untroubled region, happy alike in rulers and subjects, where he had played his peaceful part for so many sweet years. How vanished was it, though its bare outlines, its dead landscape and lineaments, were left. Its loved and honoured mistress (happiest in her lot) laid in the tomb after a wearing spell of secret sorrow that had preyed on her; its gallant young lord an exile, nameless and penniless; its time-honoured Hall deserted; its farmhouses, so well-plenished and full of comfort, invaded by poverty and disaster; its cottage-homes emptied or pinched by want; its quiet street outraged by noisy demagogues, professional agitators, and insurrectionists; its old traditions dishonoured.

Truly it was only a high sense of duty, a determination to befriend his flock in their hour of need to his utmost, that enabled the mournful rector when he pondered on these things to bear up, and prolong for a season his abode in a place which was no more the old familiar happy home, the Swardham of Rachel West and her son.

Father and daughter sat often silent for hours, desiring neither to sadden the other with the burden of heart-sickness which each bore; and then they would start to find how long the silence had lasted, and try to renew the old easy cheerful chat. But it was hard to avoid touching on some of the changes in all their surroundings. How should the atmosphere of the rectory

not be changed too? How should the
rector marvel that his child's blithe brightness had disappeared, and that the kind
eyes which met his own should lack the
frank joyousness of past years?

CHAPTER V.

BERGEN.

THE flanking mountains, thanks to which Bergen can claim to be the most picturesque town in Norway, have also a tendency which, to the thinking of some luckless visitors, out-balances their charm. Comely enough is the town, with its red-tiled roofs piled on slopes, and relieved by trees, its fringe of shipping, its suburban villas and green gardens; but when on those land-ward heights clouds brood for days, and deluges of rain obscure the rocky isles to sea-ward, blot all colour from the land-scape, rush in torrents down the streets, and hiss upon the grey sullen waters that lap the quays, then one may ungratefully wish that the bridge-spanned bay were less narrow, or its barriers more remote.

In autumn especially is Bergen subject to these long-continued rains, and little as they may affect the natives, they are found depressing by most sojourners in the place. Depressing they certainly appeared to John West, installed as he was in the best hotel, and surrounded by every creature-comfort. His crippled hands, his other burns and bruises, soon ceased to be very troublesome.

'Yours is the flesh that heals,' said the kindly doctor who tended him, 'and I only wish that my other poor patient was made of the same stuff.' And then they would quietly enter a large room, where, cased in cotton-wool and drenched with antiseptics, lay the hapless Squire of Swardham.

For days after his awfully disfigured body had been conveyed on board the Thyra to Bergen, his life had been despaired of. 'The shock to the system has been great ; he may not rally.' The doctors shook their heads over him, but did their best, and were rewarded at the end of a fortnight by his still retaining a hold on life.

'If his wounds were only in a healthier condition I should have good hope, for his will is good,' said the doctor-in-chief ; 'and he desires to live.'

Yes, Adolphus West, maimed and shriv-elled, hideously disfigured as he was, was

anxious to live ; above all, since he had
learned (in answer to the first question
he had been able to frame) that Aylmer
FitzRaymond had perished. It was from his
cousin that he heard the news, who had
accompanied him on the yacht from Bjornestrand, and had since remained by him.

He knew that to his cousin he owed his
life, saved by jeopardy of his own, and
whether or no it was from gratitude for
this service, he now desired his presence as
much as he had lately shunned it. In no
other way, however, had Adolphus shown a
change of feeling. Though his weak voice
was ever demanding aid from those bandaged
hands, he was as querulous, as thankless, as
he could have been to a mere hireling.
But of this John West, full of deep pity

and that interest which we lavish on those for whom we have risked much, made light, seeming unconscious of all hard words and ungracious ways. Adolphus, poor fellow, was not one, he thought, to be over-courteous at any time, and now, in his terrible condition of body, might be pardoned anything. If his own trifling burns were so painful, what must be the agony of one whose features were thus marred, his flesh eaten by flames? He did not know that the very extent of the injuries, the destruction of the nerves, rendered his kinsman less susceptible of pain for the present. The doctors knew, but said nothing, only assuring Jack that, as the patient so strongly desired it, his presence was absolutely essential for his chance of recovery.

Thus, in close attention to the fractious invalid, days dragged slowly on, while the rain beat on the window-panes, and the heavy sky brooded low on all outside. Jack had noticed how his cousin's spirits had improved since he was aware of Colonel FitzRaymond's death.   He recalled the rumours which had been already current when he fled from Longshire, and guessed easily at the truth ; but as no confidence was vouchsafed to him, the name of Lady Georgiana was never mentioned between them.   Only the sick man was ever pining and fretting to be taken back to England— to Swardham.   And his cousin Jack must go with him ; he should die on the journey otherwise.   This prospect was a distasteful one to poor Jack.   He would sooner have

crept again through flames than have returned thus to Swardham. Without saying
as much, he did beg hard to be excused;
he would cross the sea with Adolphus, go
with him almost to his journey's end, but
not there! not to his lost home! not to the
parish whence Mary Holbrooke must have
gone a happy bride.

But Adolphus was inexorable, he excited
himself so much over his cousin's refusal that
the doctors implored Jack to submit. And
he submitted; he bound himself by a solemn
promise not only to see his cousin safe in
Swardham Hall, but to abide there with him
for a season, till the other could do without
him. Writhing in spirit, he prayed that
this time might soon arrive, and resigned
himself, patiently and gently performing his

daily task ; suffering for want of the fresh air and exercise which in all his thirty years he had never foregone before.

Except the doctors, he saw no one with whom to exchange a word, save on two or three occasions, when he had brief interviews with Eric Bjornsen, the self-confessed gambler, whose company he had solemnly forsworn. This man's anxious face it was which he had first recognized when he revived from his swoon, to find himself laid on a homely bed in one of the cottages at Bjornestrand. His care and concern for the injured had since been infinite, both on the passage and after their arrival at the Bergen hotel. Jack had been angered with him for the recklessness which had conduced to so terrible a catastrophe, but he saw in him

such signs of sorrow and distress as removed
all traces of that displeasure. That he was
sobered and shocked by the fate of his
associate was evident, and Jack began to
hope that, late in the day as it was, this
might be the turning-point in the count's
career. When they parted finally, he could
not refuse to give the man an address where
he might write, and to echo his oft-repeated
'We must not lose sight of each other.'
It was indeed most improbable that they
should meet again, unless the count's
manner of existence should undergo some
startling transformation; but the two men
parted with mutual kindly feeling, and one
of the two resolved that the parting should
not be for ever.

After a weary while Jack's burden was

shared with a young surgeon who came out specially from England to undertake the care of the patient, especially upon the homeward journey, when such exertion should be possible. Under the skilful treatment of the new-comer, Adolphus West's case soon assumed a more hopeful aspect; and as a removal to a less rigorous climate than that of Norway in winter was judged expedient, his intense desire for return to Swardham was sooner indulged than could have been expected, considering the terrible nature of his injuries.

'There will be a certain risk, of course,' the surgeon said to Jack; 'but where a patient is set on a thing as Mr. West is set on getting home, the greater danger lies in thwarting him.'

Attempted, accordingly, and accomplished the journey was, though not till the last week of the year. The weather was fortunately propitious during the sea passage, which, by special arrangement, was made direct from Bergen to London. Here a halt of two days was necessary for rest as well as a thorough overhaul of bandages and dressings; but the patient's strength remaining good, and his longing for home becoming yet more intense as they neared it, the little *cortège* started on the third morning for Longborough.

Poor Jack was, luckily, too busy in attempting to satisfy a thousand querulous exactions to have much time for reflection. He felt himself turned into a mere machine, an automaton placed unreservedly at his cousin's disposal. What else could have taken him back than loss of his own will? Now and then he was left at peace for a minute, and then he thought of his last journey on that line—the third-class carriage, the crowded passengers, the kindly parson with his copy of the *Field*. How like a vision of the night was all that had since happened. How little he dreamed of any return, least of all in such company. As little as of the ordeals of water and of fire through which he was to be brought in safety. He dreaded the stoppage at the familiar platform of Longborough, but he dreaded in vain. The saloon in which they travelled was detached and run into a siding before the rest of the train passed into the station. No eye but those of a few respectful porters saw these privileged passengers, or the muffled form of the Squire of Swardham as it was carried to his closed carriage in the goods-yard hard by. All the arrangements of the journey had been thought out and perfectly arranged for privacy : such was the pleasure of Adolphus, and he had the wherewithal to ensure respect for his wishes.

It was dark before they reached Swardham ; but no darkness, no drawn blinds, could make much difference to John West's perception of these localities. Each turn of the road, each rise and dip, was felt by him as the carriage (the big old carriage in which he had been carried of an evening to many a neighbouring Hall) passed along. He winced and shut his eyes as the great entrance of the park was reached; truly the worst of this penance was beginning for him. His cousin had fallen into a sleep or stupor, and when at last the horses stopped at the old hall-door, he resolutely busied himself in aiding, with infinite precautions, in carrying the corpse-like form to the room, a library, prepared on the ground-floor. There was not a servant about the place whom he had ever seen before. This was a comfort. He would not let himself look about him to-night. After the long process of undressing, unbandaging, dressing the burns, feeding and laying the patient to rest—in all of which the surgeon found his assistance indispensable—he was conducted by a strange man to a little room into which he had seldom entered in the old days. Declining refreshment, he made all haste to bed, and, contrary to all expectation, sank quickly into a sound sleep beneath the good old roof-tree, which he had thought to have quitted for ever when it passed into the hands of his unknown and unloved cousin Adolphus.

CHAPTER VI.

PSYCHE, WITH A DIFFERENCE.

A DOG-CART was bowling along the road between Snugby village and Swardham, the same road along which Adolphus West had ridden Hamlet on a certain summer's day. This, however, was a winter's night, black and still, and the hour was late enough for every cottage to be shut and dark as the lamps went flashing by, and the sharp click of the hoofs and rumble of the wheels passed all unheard by tired rustic sleepers. There were

two people in the dog-cart, of whom he
who so smartly put the big brown horse
along was the Earl FitzRaymond, and the
cloaked figure beside him was his sister's.
Very much against her will had Lady
Georgiana turned out on this winter's night,
and as the brown horse trotted swiftly
on, less and less did she relish the errand
on which she was bound. But for once
'Fairy' had been obdurate, and had carried his point, as a man generally will
with an affectionate sister. Vastly as the
petulant beauty valued her limbs and those
of her only brother, she would have risked
breakage or contusion if the cart would but
have upset at some turning. There was,
however, little chance of an upset with
Fairy for driver—Fairy, who was sober as

a judge, and provokingly practical and
sententious to-night, though he had been
dining. For once his sister would have
preferred that he should have been deeper
in his cups, or even as his henchman
Captain Clancy, who ceased to have any
independent will or judgment most even-
ings by nine o'clock, and became maudlin
before midnight.

'Ugh!' shuddered the lady, 'the more
and the nearer I look at it the less I like
it, I can tell you that.'

'Well, Georgie,' the earl answered, somewhat indistinctly by reason of a cigar stump
between his teeth, 'that's irrational, child-
ish, you know. The more I look at our
financial prospect and the nearer, the less
I like it; the more thankful I feel that

there is a loophole for you, at any rate.
I am about stone-broke, that's what I
am.'

'How often have you said the same
thing?' she muttered querulously.

'Never, my dear child,' he went on,
pitching away the end of the cigar, ' with
the same awfully solemn truth. Listen :
it certainly wants two months to Lincoln,
but no improvement of the shining hour
will make my settlement there less than a
smash-up. I plunged in the autumn, back-
ing Teagown for the Handicap, as I never
plunged before. And she *was* a moral,
you know, at six stone five—only she went
amiss. But now there's no hedging ; she's
been knocked all to pieces ; slap out of the
betting, and is as good as a dead 'un. I

don't know what to back; some rank out-
sider is bound to win. So it's all U P
with this noble sportsman.'

He did not seem in the least depressed
by this melancholy prospect, and his sister
only gave vent to a short sigh or strangled
groan, as he whisked into a side entrance of
Swardham park, shaving the gate-post very
close indeed.

'Consequently, my child, you will
shortly find yourself turned loose on the
staggering luxury of—how much is it a
year?—the interest of your five thousand
pounds in the three per cents., which you
can't meddle with (why, you couldn't buy
gloves and bonnets with it!); *unless* indeed
you prefer to be mistress of all this' (he
waved his whip on either side as they sped

through the dim width of the park), 'en-
cumbered only by a man whom you can
turn round your little finger; and all the
more if he is to be a bit of an invalid.'

'A rare wife I should make to an invalid,'
she said savagely, feeling that in vouchsafing
this very visit she was in a manner com-
mitting herself to the man who awaited her.

'What is there against you?' her brother
rejoined carelessly; 'you've no debts to
speak of—'

'Because nobody would trust me then.
Ah, Fairy, let us run away together, if
your grief is so utter. Absence *hasn't* made
my heart grow fonder.'

'Fonder,' he repeated disdainfully, as he
drew up in good style at the front door of
the Hall; 'what awful rot! as if any one

expected you to be fond of a chap like that. Here' (handing her down), 'go in and win.'

If the earl, speaking from his recollection of Adolphus West as last he saw him, deemed him little likely to take a woman's fancy, what would he have said of the object now feverishly awaiting his lady love; had he beheld, without its mask of cotton wool, that ravaged face, hideously seamed and scarred, bereft of an eye, could he have sent his sister to confront it as that of her future husband? But no one outside the sick-room itself had as much as an inkling of Adolphus West's awful disfigurement, or of the nature of his indisposition. Not even his mother, though she was in the house, and had once for a moment been at the bed-side, was aware of it. The care of the remaining eye made a jealously darkened room essential, and the secret, thus religiously kept, was unsuspected by any save his medical man and his cousin. To the inquiring public it was reported that the Squire of Swardham had returned from his tour on the continent with an attack of ophthalmia; and that he had further, in his purblind state, met with an accident, a fall or strain, which prevented his moving about, even from room to room.

Mr. Clark, anxious as he was to see his patron, had to content himself with this unvarying report, and to wait till he should be summoned. And as Mr. Clark's budget was not of a particularly exhilarating or favourable sort, he brought himself to own that it must stand over till Mr. West should be in his usual health, and prayed that with convalescence an unusual amount of patience might be developed. In truth, there had been much exhaustion, and some renewed suffering, since the arrival at the Hall.

'We ought to have stayed a full week in London,' said Hale the surgeon, 'only he is so plaguey pig-headed (if you'll excuse the expression) that he would have fretted himself into a fever. Now he clamours for anodynes, and I dare not give him half as much chloral as he wants. If it were not for your help, Mr. West, and that your patience makes me ashamed of myself, I could hardly carry the case on.'

Poor Jack, living on thorns, desperately

binding himself down to his task, pained and stirred by every inanimate object around him, felt himself little deserving of praise.

'Do go out, Mr. West, while he is unconscious, at any rate ; you look ill, and the air will do you good.'

Jack was indeed sickening for fresh air and a good stretch ; but, oh ! not in Swardham park. He made light of his own doings and his own looks, and strove to encourage the sturdy surgeon, who was indeed, spite of occasional grumbling, doing his best for his patient.

At last, on the sixth day after the arrival in Longshire, Adolphus West, waking from a long sleep late in the afternoon, pronounced himself much better, almost well, in fact. Though the early twilight of January was already darkening into night, the Squire of Swardham insisted on despatching an immediate message to Beausite, in which he implored his adored one to crown and celebrate his recovery by coming over to see him at once, 'evening being his best time,' he said. His communications with Lady Georgiana had been of the scantiest since his 'trifling accident,' as he was pleased to term it. He could not write, and did not choose to employ his cousin as amanuensis. He had, however, while still at Bergen, found means of informing the lady that she was a widow, adding that he would tell her more when he came to claim his reward. Now he felt that the time had come. She had not written to him ; she had often declared that she never wrote to any one but her dressmaker.

This did not discourage his ardour ; he felt sure that she must melt to one who had been brave in her cause, suffering as he had suffered.   And as to his disfigurement, the hideousness of which he imperfectly realized, he had a plan to guard against shocking her at first.   After a while, after they were married, she would, so he told himself, think none the worse of him for those scars.   Those about him had had a bad time of it since the messenger returned from Beausite, bringing a short note from the earl.   ' His sister was out,' he said, ' and though she would be home before seven, they had guests whom they could hardly leave.   Under the circumstances, however, they would start as soon after dinner as possible, and hoped to be at Swardham by ten o'clock.'

In expectation of this visit Adolphus so fidgetted, that the exasperated surgeon often assured him that, unless he controlled his excitement, he would certainly be too ill to see any one. No detail, however, in the arrangement of the sofa, to which he insisted on being transferred, or of the rest of his properties, including a dressing-gown of quilted satin in which his bandaged limbs were draped, was so small as to escape anxious pondering, for the production of the best effect. Every trace of a sick room must be banished; fragrant pastilles must be burned in suffocating profusion; above all, the shaded lights must be so disposed as not to alarm a visitor by too great obscurity, and yet to reveal no more of the principal figure than his outline. All had to be rehearsed over and over again. The visitor must be shown to a chair just *there!*—all other seats were to be banished to the dimmest corners lest a mistake should be possible. He made his cousin again and again sit down in this chair, and put him on his honour to describe accurately the effect of his studied pose as he reclined. Would a person, a lady for instance, who had not seen him for some time, be able to see any difference in him? Ought the cushions to be raised or lowered? Was the room so dark as to frighten any one? A hundred anxious questions were poured out to which Jack

did his best to return soothing answers.
From his soul he pitied this poor agitated
creature, with his half mask of thin cotton-
wool through which one eye peeped gro-
tesquely, beneath an embroidered cap of
velvet. Surely a woman's heart might be
touched, even if her eyes were sharp
enough to penetrate the semi-gloom. The
hours lagged slowly, and the invalid was
fain piteously to beseech for cordials to keep
him up.

'This is the rankest folly,' growled Hale
the surgeon, determining that he would
admit no more untimely visitors.

'You promised me! you promised me!'
Adolphus gasped. 'Don't go further than
the next room when they come. I may
want you—both of you.'

At length came the sound of wheels, of the opening door, of steps and voices in the paved hall, and in another minute the brother and sister were ushered into the room.

'Hallo! old fellow!' such was Lord FitzRaymond's playful salutation; 'this is blind man's holiday! Moses with the candle out was nothing to this!—where are you?'

He advanced warily as he spoke, a tall gallant figure in his 'pink' dress-coat with button of the Longshire hunt, and white waistcoat; but the master of the house had no eyes for the earl. In her brother's wake Lady Georgiana softly followed; her arms wrapped in a white opera cloak, the rose-lined hood of which was half slipping from her dark hair. As he fixed his passionate gaze on her, Adolphus thought her more lovely than ever. How exquisite the grace of her movements! How those beautiful startled eyes shone as she faced the shaded lamp behind his sofa! He tingled all over his poor marred frame as he beheld her, and thought that he had fairly won her for his own. If those eyes were bright with apprehension—if that bosom heaved with repugnance—if those full red lips were silent because they could find no greeting— he knew it not in his short ecstasy. Something he murmured, devouring her the while with his gaze, about an honour which he never could forget, and then there fell a silence on the group, till FitzRaymond, standing behind his sister's chair, with a comical glance around, proposed to take himself off 'to any place where he could have his cigarette.'

'I sha'n't be gone five minutes,' he said, as he pulled his cuff away from her detaining hand, patting her slyly on the shoulder as he did so.

'Not there then,' said Adolphus, as the earl made for the door by which he had entered; 'the door behind you!—you'll find two gentlemen and more light than suits me—and you will be within call,' he added, wishing to reassure his silent visitor.

The door shut and silence reigned anew. His heart beat till he fancied that she must hear its throbs above such sounds as broke the stillness, the tinkling of cinders falling on the hearth, the muffled drone of talking in the next room.

'You know that you are free,' he whispered at last, leaning as much toward her as he dared.

'Yes, I know,' she said.

Her lips felt dry and her voice sounded harshly to herself : she felt as though toils were closing round her, and that there was no longer any escape for her. He could touch her with his outstretched arm, and now he tried very gently to find her hand, still muffled in the folds of the cloak, as he went on :

'Free to marry me, without anything of that law-business beforehand—without anything from which you shrank :' she shrank nevertheless under his touch and said once more :

'Yes, I know.'

'Then, why,' he murmured passion-
ately, 'why, knowing this, refuse me this
hand ?'

As she clenched the hand beneath her
cloak, her brother's laugh, jovial, almost
boyish, reached her ear through the intervening door. Ah, reckless fellow, sporting
on the brink of ruin, and always so unfit
to take care of himself!—who but she could
influence him, and of what use her influence
—unless. Her hand came suddenly from
under the cloak and surrendered itself to
the frantic pressure of the feverish fingers
which caught it.

'Darling!' he moaned, half stupefied by
his bliss—'my own darling!'

His swimming head sank back on the
cushions. One moment to recover himself,

and he would tell her all his plans. He had thought it all out so often in his painful sleepless hours! He would surprise her into a hasty, perhaps immediate, marriage. While in London he had actually made Hale procure him a special license—under which, by the expenditure of twenty guineas, no restrictions of time or place would impede the ceremony. All seemed to be going as he desired! Of course she was nervous, agitated—any woman would be that—but willing, oh! manifestly willing! Why should she leave the house this night unwedded? Why should she ever leave the house? Mr. Holbrooke or some other parson could be fetched in half an hour, and there were plenty of witnesses! All this flashed through his mind as he still

held her unresponsive hand. Stammering
with eagerness he began to propound his
scheme, while she hearkened dumb and
passive. Why not? Why not? Would it
be better to bear a month hence or a week
hence? On the other hand, would not delay
make Fairy's extrication from that coming
ordeal more difficult? To marry this man,
and then not be in time to rescue her
brother—that would be awful! She had all
her life defied conventionalities—why not
startle the ranks she despised, all the Clan
Grundy, by one more eccentricity? Emboldened by her tacit acquiescence he
stopped to kiss her hand, designing presently to summon those in the next room,
when suddenly the door by which his
visitors had entered was flung open, and

a woman's figure, short, stout, and trembling with emotion, stood on the threshold, letting the candle which she carried shine full upon his face.

Old Mrs. Van Lennep had retired, according to her wont, at ten o'clock that evening. She was not wanted in that house—that she felt keenly, and meditated departure on the morrow. She was folding some dresses to be packed when she heard the noises attendant on the entry of Lord FitzRaymond and his sister. Surprised and curious, she stepped from her chamber, and peering over the balustrade beheld a lady and gentleman doffing their wraps in the hall, and presently disappearing in the direction of her son's room—that room from which her motherly presence was all but banished. To descend

to the room of her friend the housekeeper
was her sole resource; perhaps Milligan
might know what had not been confided to
her master's mother. Milligan knew well
enough, short as the interval had been for
gaining the knowledge, who the intruders
were. Now she understood why Joseph
had been sent galloping to Beausite!—
why there had been a clearance of phials
and compresses in master's room! It
was extraordinary, she quite agreed—still,
they had *both* been shown in. After some
friendly chat, wherein a low opinion of fast
ladies in general and of one in particular
was freely broached, Mrs. Van Lennep
retreated to her chamber once more, while
Milligan felt it her duty to make a little
tour. In ten minutes the housekeeper rushed

into the old woman's room in high excitement. She had it from the upper house-
maid that Thomas had just taken spirits
and soda-water into the smoking-room,
where he had found *three* of them, the lord
as well as the 'two doctor men.' They
were alone then, her Dolf and this woman,
neither maid, wife, nor widow. Closeted
together at an hour when proper people
were seeking their beds! But they were
reckoning without one person in the house.

On to her feet bounced the old lady,
speechless with wrath. Catching up her
candlestick she brushed by Milligan, and
paused not till she had flung open the
forbidden door. There she stood on the
threshold, all shaking, but aghast at the
countenance (she scarce knew *whose*) on

which her light fell full. The velvet cap
had slipped over one ear, pulling with it a
deep green shade ; the mask of cotton wool
which had covered the upper part of the
face hung loose, and in all their horrid
unsightliness, patched scalp, eyeless cavity,
ulcerous cheek were illuminated. On the
lips of this death's-head still played the
smirk of ineffable gratification, far uglier
there than the grin of any fleshless skull.
In one instant, while the old woman shrank
appalled, dropping the candlestick to the
ground, the room rang with Lady Georgiana's
shrieks. The next, the further door was
violently opened and Lord FitzRaymond
rushed to his sister's side, followed by
Hale and John West. The keen eyes of
the surgeon scanned the room, the open

door and the faltering figure of the old woman, and at once comprehended the situation.

'Take me away! take me this moment from this awful room—from this house! I shall die if I stop a moment—if I ever had to return!' screamed Lady G., clinging to her brother.

'What's all this?' the earl began, with a furious scowl. 'Has yonder dog—"

'No,' interrupted Hale, 'he hasn't. He has done nothing more than making an exhibition of a head-piece which is a trifle damaged—not so handsome as it used to be.' He muttered something more into Lord FitzRaymond's ear.

'Oh,' said the peer sheepishly, 'I'm awfully sorry, West; and Georgie will be sorry when she understands,—won't you, Georgie ? '

He tried to lead her nearer to the pros-trate figure on the sofa as he spoke ; but she broke from him violently, and in high, quivering tones cried out :

'No, never again, come what may !   It made me sick, do you hear ?   It makes me sick now.   I should swoon with loathing if he ever touched me again, and that is my last word to him.   Fairy, take me away at once, as you are a gentleman.'

The wild disgust, the intensity of horror, expressed in her utterance, was indescrib-able.   There was no hushing, no soothing, or gainsaying possible.   Abashed and speechless, her brother led her from the room.   As the door closed behind them the sound of Mrs. Van Lennep's sobs was alone to be heard.

'Oh, my boy!' she moaned; 'oh, my only living child!—what have they done to you? But your mother loves you all the same—your poor mother that you would not see, though for that wicked woman you could lose your rest; and'——

Here Adolphus, who had lain as one stunned, hiding his unhappy features amid the pillows, burst into wild yells and curses.

'It was you, hag—wretch—she-devil!— you, with your meddling pretence of love, who spoiled all.'

As he raved, John West pushed the forlorn, weeping mother to the door.

'He is delirious, you must not heed him.

We will fetch you when he is himself again.'

He turned the key on her at last, and ran to help Hale. The miserable patient, in a paroxysm of frenzy, had rolled from the sofa to the floor, and was madly tearing the bandages from his wounds. The two men had an awful time of it; for the puny, wasted form seemed to develop terrible strength, and it was a hard struggle, and not a wholly successful one, to prevent his inflicting on himself the most serious hurt. At last a handkerchief soaked in ether and chloroform was forcibly held to his mouth and nostrils, and his wild writhings and hideous cries subsided till all was still, and he could be put to bed.

'And a fine wreck he has made of himself,' said Hale the surgeon, gloomily. ' But it is partly my fault too. Why did I give in to admitting visitors ? '

' He said you promised him.'

Jack spoke wearily, for he was worn out.

' Well, it has been all his cry whenever he has had me alone, all along. " You *must* get me well enough to meet my bride as soon as ever we get home," he used to say. He made me buy a special license for him in London,—just think of that !—and a ring,—I give you my word,—and all kinds of humbug I had to palaver before they would let me have the license. That was her shoe which he kept under his pillow. You must have seen it, though he didn't mumble and kiss it before you. Good Lord ! a nice figure-head his is for a bride-

groom! I can't be sorry that his precious
scheme was spoiled, for to cheat a handsome woman into such a marriage would
have been too disgraceful, unless they could
have lived ever after on the terms of Cupid
and his young woman—Psyche, wasn't her
name? And I remember *that* didn't last
long. But, by Jove! that uncommonly
pretty creature who was removed in hys-
terics, or something very near, would have
envied Psyche in the same predicament.
Cupid took himself off for good and all as
soon as his missus set eyes on him; your
cousin would not have had so much grace,
he would have stuck where he was, an
obstinate and awkward fact for daylight.
The modern Psyche is too wary though. She
has bolted, and left her swain disconsolate.'

The surgeon chuckled over his classical conceit, but met with no response. John West's head had dropped on his arms as he sat at a table, and he was sound asleep.

CHAPTER VII.

DARKEST HOUR BEFORE THE DAWN.

'NEVER, I tell you, never! if all the earth were united to believe it and proclaim it, we in Swardham know better! It's no use bringing among us such a charge against John West. We know him too well, and we would scorn to alter our faith, just because he is not here to clear himself.'

It was Mary Holbrooke, flushed and trembling, all unlike patient Griselda to behold, who thus raised her clear sweet voice, shrilling in unwonted excitement.

Standing in her own pretty drawing-room, she faced fat Lady Woollett, who extended two black-gloved hands in deprecation as she listened; and for answer only made a moan of perplexity.

'My dear,' she said at last, with an anxious peep up at those fair knitted brows, 'my dear, it makes me miserable, I'm sure. My poor Mr. Fife's own niece, you understand, and a staid girl as ever lived, poor thing, and thoroughly well off too. If she has not been made away with, where is she? think of that. And if he had nothing to do with it, why don't he come forward and say so? What between Sir Tancred, who won't hear a word, and is angrier with us all than I could have believed possible, and all the Fifes, and my own brother, who

won't allow there can be a doubt, I'm
nearly distracted; and if you or your dear
father *could* have thrown any light on Mr.
West's proceedings, to clear him, of course,
no one would be more glad of it than I.'

The poor lady wiped away a tear and
shook her plumed bonnet dolorously.

'Lady Woollett,' Mary resumed in her
usual tones, 'I know you have a kind
heart, and Sir Tancred, God bless him! he
is a true friend. I only wish, ah! *how* I
wish we could tell you where to find Mr.
West. But we cannot listen to your
brother's suggestion with common patience.
Mr. West is the soul of honour,—any one
in the county could tell you that,—and to
connect him with anything clandestine, and
worse, would be wrong and wicked if it

were not absurd. Depend upon it, he knows no more of Miss Fife's disappearance than I do; dismiss such a notion from your mind, you that have seen him and know his history.'

'Then, my dear,' said the visitor, solemnly, 'it must be that some dreadful accident has happened, and one or both of them have lost their lives. You don't know what a country it is; I never could bear it myself. There are places where scores of poor creatures might perish unknown—crags and rocks, and quaking bogs. Oh, why did the poor girl choose to live in such a desert? Depend upon it, she has met her death there, and perhaps he was killed in trying to save her.'

Mary felt her knees knock together as

this gloomy description of the dangers of Ross-shire was unfolded. Was it more comforting to think of him as dead, laid in some awful ravine, or sunk in some morass, than even as the partner of this girl's flight? But she was outwardly brave and incredulous.

'Nay,' she said, 'there are other ways of accounting for a person's disappearance, surely many other ways.'

She stopped, chilled by inward dread.

'Aye,' rejoined Lady Woollett, 'for one person, and that a man, to have suddenly gone away; but two, a young man and a young woman, both in one hour—if they are not together in life, they are not far apart in death, I sadly fear. Well, my dear' (after a pause), 'forgive me for having

pained you; it was my duty to inquire of
you; but as no light is cast on this mystery
I will be going, with a heavy heart. The
Fifes are anxiously expecting a letter from
me, but it's little I have to tell. Good-bye,
my dear, good-bye. And you'll not be
annoyed with them, nor with my brother,
when you reflect what an awkward position
Hilda's kith and kin are in; they are in
the right to leave no stone unturned.
Though in my opinion it will be a sorrowful
satisfaction, if they come at the bottom of
the matter, still.'

The good garrulous soul had talked herself out of the room at last, and Mary was
left alone to digest her strange and unwelcome tidings.

John West a sort of gamekeeper to one

of these Fifes!—that might have been a sufficiently distasteful fact to swallow, for in her inexperience, her romantic innocence, she had pictured her hero as already half-way up the steps to fame, though in what special profession she had not made up her mind. But she bestowed only a passing thought on this first surprise, merged as it was and lost in what lay behind. Her lover, the man who had strained her to his breast in that garden outside (a sacred spot thenceforth), accused of an elopement with his employer's niece, and suspected of subsequent foul play! that stainless name bandied on the coarse lips of such as Mr. Auchmuty, and associated with she scarce knew what crime! Oh, it was horrible; but it was at any rate false, false and baseless calumny.

What, however, if Lady Woollett's bodings should not be equally baseless! What if the destiny under which John West had lost mother, home, fortune, place in the world, were indeed relentless and unsated, and had exacted yet another fine—all that was left to him—even his life!

Mary had fancied herself sad enough, hopeless enough in her true love before Lady Woollett's brougham stopped, a messenger of fate, at the rectory door. But what is the burden of hope deferred compared with the survivor's anguish when death has intervened between two parted lovers? Was he never to know then how constant she had been? Had he gone down to a nameless grave ignorant and unconsoled? The poor girl broke down under her new terror, feeling that she no longer cared to show a bold front to her little world.

The rector was in London, whither he had gone on the day previous in the interests of the Everett family. He had suggested to the ruined farmer that, rather than see his sons 'work for wage,' he might allow the young men at least to emigrate. The plan had been adopted with ardour, and as the stalwart yeomen seemed to look to him for the initiative in each necessary step, the rector made an appointment with a colonial agent, and took himself off to town for three days.

Mary had longed for her father's support when first Lady Woollett had opened her arraignment. His indignation would have been equal to her own, and he could (so she thought) have rebutted this disgraceful imputation far more effectually.

Now, however, that the glow of excitement had passed she was thankful to be alone with that sad heart which must not be eased by confidence. She could not for a while continue the usual routine of her life and of the house. In her father's absence it was betraying nothing, shirking no duty, to collapse, to proclaim herself unwell, her meals and her housewifely functions in abeyance till further notice. She would give herself the time until her father's return for unrestrained indulgence of her misery. After that dear father should have rejoined her, she would force herself to rise, and eat and drink ; to order dinner and take interest in the parish—all as before. That she would find no such excessive joyousness in the rector's mood as to jar with her own she was well aware. He was never merry of late, and when he heard of these slanders, and of his old pupil's prolonged disappearance, he would be both agitated and anxious in the extreme.

So Mary crept up-stairs to her room, leaving the warm pretty drawing-room to solitude, and lay down on her bed. The neat parlour-maid soon found her there, and heard her injunctions.

'No doctor ; nothing at all till she rang ; then only tea. At home to no one. No ; it was not exactly a headache ; it was just that she was not quite herself and best alone.'

'Dear, dear,' said the maid when she reached the kitchen. 'Miss does look like death, and with master away; I *should* like to have in the doctor, but I dursn't; she don't want no doctor, she says.'

The servants were justly fond of their young mistress, but were not proof against the joys of an unexpected holiday. Miss particularly desired to be left in peace, and food she turned against. So cook embraced the occasion to go 'up-street' and visit a crony, and the other two had a very pleasant afternoon making up new bonnets, till cook returned and gave them crumpets and a turnover for tea.

The bell had never rung, but Anne took up a cup of tea, and returned rather penitent for a few minutes.

'She ain't looking no better; I don't know what master will say.'

But, as cook observed, often a night's rest had made *her* all right when she had been never-so at bed-time. Youth and high spirits soon prevailed, and the sufferer was forgotten. Cook's friend, the baker's wife up-street, was keeping her birthday that evening, and had said how glad she should be to see any of the rectory servants. There would be quite a party, with games and mulled elder wine. Cook generously offered to mind the house while the other two went a pleasuring. But this the others would not hear of.

At last it was agreed that cook should go too, just for half-an-hour, taking the back-door key in her pocket. Thus when about nine o'clock Mary, forbidden to sleep by the disquiet of her innocent breast, that teemed with presentiments of precipices and abysses, and all manner of lairs of sudden death, conceived a sudden hatred of her bed, and came softly down-stairs again, she found the house deserted, though a light in the hall and another in the kitchen were tokens of the desertion being but temporary.

'I ought to scold them,' Mary thought, 'but I shall be up-stairs again presently. I need not reveal that I know. Ah! there is one of them returning; rather impudent of her to come in by the study.'

The door of the rector's study was open, and the light in the hall shone into the room. Mary stood to see which of her domestics was taking the liberty of entering

by the door-window, sacred to her father
and his particular friends.

With quick alarm, and most unpleasant
realizing that she was alone in the house,
she saw a tall man's figure pass into the
room.   Noiselessly she turned to flee up
the stairs, designing to lock herself into her
room and scream from the window, when
she heard a voice.

'Holbrooke! rector! where are you?' it
said softly.

Once more Mary turned, her heart beating
furiously, her ears strained to catch another
word.   But it was needless, she was quite
sure.   Whether it belonged to a living
man or to a disembodied spirit, that voice
was John West's.   He was in the study,
calling for her father

Scarce knowing what she did, unconscious of her limbs or gait, she went straight into the half-lit room, where, sure enough, there was the figure seated in her father's chair. Right up to it she walked, trembling but resolute.

'My father is away,' she said quietly; 'but I heard you call, and knew your voice directly.'

Any nervous terrors which had been present to her, fostered by the ominous talk of the morning, and her unprotected and disconsolate state, went from her as she spoke her little ordinary sentence. She could hear the quickened breathing of him who sat in the chair, and fearlessly she laid a little hand on his, where it rested on the chair-arm.

As it was grasped by that other hand,
warm and powerful, a great flood of thankfulness rushed over her and swept away all
trouble, all discomfort of body or mind.
Her very joy took away all command of
words. All she could do, as he remained
still silent, was to repeat,

'My father is away; could I do as
well?'

It was a little formula familiar to Mary,
often used when poor people called in the
rector's absence, who usually found that
Mary 'did' very well indeed. And this
poor fellow—what did he make of the
rector's substitute? Hoarsely he whispered,
holding still the little hand,

'Not married, Mary?' He could feel
even by her hand how she shook her head,

her whole person, in dissent. 'Not going to be, Mary? not engaged?' There was a pause, and no shaking this time.

He breathed harder than ever as he thought 'must he loose this hand for ever,' after the next sentence. But then a voice, divinely soft and sweet, answered him,—

'I thought myself engaged once, just for one happy night. But in the morning I was told not to think so. That was by a letter; but, do you know, I have not felt as though pen and ink could undo what had been, and till the writer tells me that I am a little silly girl for my pains (as I dare say I am), I shall never think that engagement quite ended, certainly never, *never* think of any one else.'

Had it been daylight, even good candlelight, Mary Holbrooke could hardly have delivered herself of that which was in her ingenuous heart. Amid blushes she would have broken down in the first sentence. Aye, and had she not known, as recently she had known, of this man's descent in the world's scale, of his living by his daily labour, of his being now beset by slanders and imputations, she might have been far more reticent and coy, even in that dim room But in her deep love for him, she felt that in his adversity any coyness might be misconstrued, and so she gave him the truth in the simple words which came first, faltering, but ringing very true.

First let her comfort him with all the comfort that love could give him ; then for the dispersion into thin air of this wretched false story. He should see her perfect love and trust before she as much as asked a question as to his marvellous arrival in this old familiar spot.

And did she succeed in her guileless plan? As Jack West rose, before her last word was well uttered, as he clasped her to his beating heart, he swore to himself in his transport that all else was well lost for the rapture of this moment. Ah! it was well that cook had yielded to those seductive games, that cheering cup of mulled elder wine. The other maidens vowed and declared that Miss Mary would sooner have their room than their company on this particular evening, and, for a wonder, these truant women were right.

Revel, jovial cook, in thy run of good

luck at 'all-fours'; laugh your loudest, light-hearted house and parlour-maids at the witticisms of attentive village swains. Your gaiety is timely, your absence inspired ; your young mistress will say nothing if you keep it up till the midnight chime. It was not till the end of a short sweet hour, that ran by without a misgiving, and healed every furrow of the past, that Jack roused himself with a start.

'But, my dearest, my own, I came here to persuade your father, whom I thought I should be sure to find alone here, to come with me to my cousin's sick-room. He is so very ill that he ought to see a clergyman ; and as the Hall servants are strangers, and seem to know nothing of the rectory, I came myself, meaning to be quite secret and unrecognized by any one but the good rector.'

Mary was by this time such a very different creature to the Mary of the morning, of many mornings past, that she actually laughed, a little happy trill, as she replied,

'I ought to beg many pardons for interfering with such an excellent plan; and I ought *not* to laugh if Mr. West is so ill; but, you see, it couldn't be helped; I suppose it was to be.'

Ah, yes; of doubts and difficulties frowning on them as darkly as ever she recked nothing at all. Her weary waiting was over; her constant loyalty justified. 'It was to be.' He was actually going at last, after how many false starts and delicious delays,

before she thought to ask him whether he
could satisfy the anxiety of a good neighbour, and of a whole clan of Fifes in
the distance, by revealing aught as to a
missing lady, one Miss Hilda Fife? So
serene was her mood, so perfect her content, that she could put this question, after
all the morning's wretchedness, almost
lightly. He started violently, and she
saw a spasm of pain contract his brow
(they were now in the lighted hall) as he
replied,—

'Good heavens! I wrote six weeks ago—
wrote when it was pain and grief to me
to write, to her London relatives' address,
telling them of that unhappy creature's
melancholy fate. How can they possibly
have failed to get my letter?' Then in

answer to Mary's awed look of inquiry he went on,—'It hurts me to speak of such a thing to-night, Mary, but Hilda Fife was drowned—drowned at sea the night after her uncle's funeral, and I alone witnessed it. And her people have never heard! Surely they don't—'

He looked down at the sweet face nestling against his shoulder.

'Ah! no matter,' she said, 'what they have thought; all will be plain now, though how sad, how miserable—'

'Don't think about it,' he said with energy; 'God knows there was none to blame but herself. But this is no time to tell a painful story; it must be told in the proper quarter without delay. I will write again. Let no shadow rest on our good-bye to-night, Mary.' There was no shadow on the trustful, candid face which he kissed fondly. 'The rector will have a fine account to settle with me when he learns of all this.'

'If anything could make his joy in recovering you more deep,' she murmured bashfully, 'I think it would be this.'

CHAPTER VIII.

AS IT WAS MEANT TO BE.

'ERYSIPELAS has set in.' Such was Hale's curt answer, next morning early, to John West's inquiries after the invalid. 'Yes,' he added; 'I have sent for Turner, the Longborough swell, and telegraphed for a still greater swell to London; it's proper in the case of a wealthy patient; but, upon my word, I don't believe there can be the slightest doubt, or, for the matter of that, the slightest chance.'

This sentence of doom came as a shock

upon the hearer. His kinsman was not one whom he could love or respect, but he was still young, and had only lately entered on the enjoyment of a fine position and corresponding income. That from these he had himself been ousted in this cousin's favour found no place in his present thoughts. It was hard to die; was there indeed no hope?

With that unperturbed and matter-of-fact way which is not callousness, though sometimes imputed as such to medical men, the surgeon explained to him something of the nature of the newly-developed disease, and discussed the probabilities in this case in particular.

'There has been delirium, which may recur, or, owing to the great exhaustion, he

may go off without another acute attack.
In either case the odds are that there will
be no conscious interval. We didn't think
when he was fussing about the smartening
up of the room for his visitors, that we
were listening to his last sensible remarks,
eh ? '

' Poor fellow ! poor fellow ! do you think
that he would have pulled through if
all that unfortunate business had been
avoided ? '

' It's hard to say ; partly depends on
what you mean by pulling through.   In
my opinion he could never have had any
satisfaction out of his life, but he might
have lived after a fashion, perhaps for some
years.'

' A devoted woman's love might have

made his life bearable,' Jack said, out of
his full heart.

Hale raised his eyebrows as he replied,—

'I'm afraid the woman he was set on
wasn't just that style. She'd have had to
"make believe very hard," like the immortal
marchioness. Well, as you're ready to
relieve me, I'll get a few hours' sleep.
No immediate change is likely.'

In the course of the day both doctors
arrived, the distinguished provincial and
the yet more eminent Londoner. There
was a formal consultation; but, as Hale
had anticipated, nothing was added to his
diagnosis but two confirmatory opinions.

Mr. Clark was in waiting with two
cheques, and the two great men returned
to catch up their arrears of engagements,

leaving the young surgeon and his amateur assistant to watch the running down of the mortal machinery. All through the afternoon the condition of coma and collapse was unchanged.

'There will be no return of consciousness,' Hale repeated, who was surprised that the sands of life drained away so slowly.

At ten o'clock John West was again alone with the dying man, having persuaded Hale to go to bed, whence he was to be called 'if there was any change.' Poor old Mrs. Van Lennep had also retired, worn out with hours of weeping and piteous prayer. Since her son had, in his bitterness of soul, reviled and even cursed her, she had been utterly crushed, and could do nothing but cry inconsolably. Better, she thought, the least prosperous days in Britannia Street than this grandeur which had corroded her boy's heart, and exposed him to what was like to be his death.

Left alone in the silent room, John West strove to attune his thoughts to the solemnity of the situation. If the rector returned, as Mary had expected, he was to come over to the Hall at once. He still might come if he travelled by the down mail, and his old pupil yearned to see his kind face, and hear his reverent voice in the prayers for the departing soul.

Though his newly-secured happiness as Mary's lover encompassed him as with a warm and elastic garb of well-being, he would not permit his thoughts to luxuriate in detail amid his joys, or to attempt to unravel the still tangled maze of his future life. Neither his mother nor his grand-sire had in their last hours admitted of such a watch as now he was keeping by his cousin's bed-side. The old squire had expired of sheer old age, in his elbow-chair. The manner of Rachel West's summons has been described in these pages.

It was the first death-bed by which John West had sat, and it was with awe that he watched the heavings of the wave of life, already so faint and feeble. But for hours there was no change.

'He has lived into another day,' the watcher thought, as he rose to stretch his chilled feet to the fire.

As he stood on the hearth he heard a faint whisper of his own name, 'John.' A hurried glance convinced him that his cousin, contrary to Hale's prophecy, was awake and apparently conscious, and he bent over him with eager sympathy. It was almost as though the words came from one already beyond the veil. But the faint syllables were, as it seemed, of no solemn import, only,

'My dressing-bag.'

He fetched the smart morocco bag which had accompanied Adolphus on his travels, emblazoned with crest and monogram, and set it on the chair by the bed-side, on which he had been sitting. It was locked, and he turned inquiringly to Adolphus, who motioned with his head upwards. In a fob there hung the sick man's watch, and taking it out, John found a key upon the chain. He could see that he was doing right; and unlocking the bag, paused for further direction.

'Paper in the pocket,' Adolphus murmured.

Feeling among the silver-topped bottles and fittings of the bag, he soon found the pocket, and in it a folded paper, which he held before his cousin's face, on which a strange excitement now appeared.

'Burn — burn it!' Adolphus said, in much louder tones.

But, as the other stood up to obey, he saw the endorsement on the paper. It was a will—his cousin's will. Staying his hand, he started back.

'Adolphus,' he said, 'I cannot destroy your will. It would not be right.'

The poor blurred features worked terribly, and the head rolled on the pillow—the limbs already powerless.

'You must! you must!' he gasped; 'I know what I am about.'

'Let me fetch Clark then, he is in the house,' said John, dismayed, and keeping the document fast.

'Ah!' a long-drawn, piteous sigh; 'I am so faint—give me wine.'

There was a liqueur-case on a side-table, and a glass of green Chartreuse was soon held to those dry lips, that drained it eagerly.

'Stay where you are,' Adolphus resumed more firmly: 'by that will *she* gets everything—she who sat there and cried, 'It

makes me sick,' and fled from me as from
the plague. Ah, cruel! cruel!—she broke my
heart. Burn it, and all shall be yours, as
it was meant to be. Do you understand me?'

Understand him! Good heavens! did he
not understand. In one lightning flash he
saw all: as it *was*, if this will stood:
a stranger—and *such* a stranger!—enriched
by all the broad lands of the Wests, turning
his mother's house into a second Beausite:
as it might be if Adolphus died intestate,
the loss and suffering of the last two
years erased, himself restored to that proud
inheritance, a softened, chastened man,
blessed with the love of his mother's
cherished little Mary.

Of the fierce temptation of that moment
he never could think without a throe.

There was no detail of either fortune which was spared him, vivid and real, as he stood unnerved and anguished by the ordeal. Was it not right and just and equitable that he should succeed? But ah! the slur, the damning slur that would attach to such succession! The will's existence must transpire; and who would believe his true account of the matter, who not credit him with deep design, fostered by his cousin's weakness, culminating in the will's destruction?

'Ah! you will do it? I thought you would.'

Was there a slight tinge of contempt in the triumph of that faintly panted sentence? Ere it was finished the tempted man had won the battle.

'Less than before, cousin, is it possible to do as you ask,' he said gently but resolutely, and laid the will upon the pillow. 'If you order me I will fetch Clark at once : that is all I can do.'

The dying man uttered a low terrible cry.

'Too late! it will be too late! Burn it! burn it now!'

His lips parted for more words, but could not frame them. The feeble breath could do no more than blow idle bubbles from that working mouth. And then in the throat began, harsh and quick, the warning rattle. But still there was a pleading gaze in the eye that sought the watcher's eyes.

So urgent was the moment that, reluctant

as he was to leave the room, Jack flew to where Hale slept, near at hand, and shaking him, bid him rouse Mrs. Van Lennep and Clark and hurry them to the bed-side. But when he returned Adolphus was in the last agony. He had caught the paper between his teeth, worrying it in his baffled hatred of its purport, striving to rend and deface it with its expiring efforts.

It was a harrowing spectacle; but quickly the will dropped from the falling jaw, dented and gnawed and slavered, but un-revoked. And from the dead man's breast Mr. Clark removed it into the jealous custody of the law, while yet the sobbing mother knelt at the bed-side, and the two men who had tended the frail still frame stood by, with prayers upon their lips.

Then there was a slight stir at the room door and the rector advanced, on tip-toe, to find himself too late to execute his solemn errand of commending to its Maker and Judge the passing soul.

The mail train had been delayed many hours on its road that night by the break-down of its engine. No sooner had Mr. Holbrooke reached home than his daughter, relieved from an anxious vigil, despatched him to the Hall. The good man's amazed joy when he heard that beside the new squire's sick bed he would find his loved pupil, whom still in his heart he recognized as the true squire, may well be imagined.

Even in the awe with which he presently learned that Adolphus West had passed away was mingled the thankfulness of his heart.

Even in that chamber, where he strove
to console the stricken mother of the dead
man, he could scarcely repress the rapture
of welcoming John West to his own again.
For now surely there could be no doubt!
Leaving neither widow nor child, the sole
descendant in the male line of the old
squire had died, and who should bar the
right of Rachel West's son, the true des-
tined heir of Swardham, the noble-looking
man who, sad and subdued, worn as though
by a weary struggle with adversity, surrendered his hand to the clasp of his oldest
friend ?

Almost in silence John West agreed to
Mr. Holbrooke's proposal that he should
quit the Hall with him and take up his
abode for the present at the rectory. With

short delay the two friends were crossing the park. They could find their way to the rectory blindfold, and in the early hours of this winter's day it was well for them that such was the case. Once in the open air, and alone with his old pupil, the rector could not keep down the hopeful tumult of his breast.

'Oh, my dear boy,' he said tremulously, 'God pardon me for seeming to rejoice in the death of a young man, and one of the Wests; but how can I weigh it against all that's on the other side? Such indignity as it has been for you; such suffering and woe for Swardham; enough to make the old squire come back from a better place. And now it will all be righted; you have come to your own again. I have never wished your dear mother among us again till this hour.'

Lost in his prospects of recovered felicity for his parish, the rector could find no space for inquiring whence his friend had come, or how he chanced to be in attendance on his cousin. It was enough that he was at home among his own loyal people again, who would welcome him with ecstasy.

John West's heart was wrung as his old friend's faltering sentences fell on his ears. It might have been. All this happiness for all these well-loved folks might indeed have been dawning with this wintry dawn. Adolphus had certainly wished in his last moments that so it should be.

'As it was meant to be,' he had said, acknowledging the perversity of the fortune

which had enriched him at his cousin's ex-
pense, as well as the propriety of restoring
to him, with his dying breath, that whereof
mischance had bereft him. But this view
had developed too late. It had needed
the sting of wounded love, the sickness
of repulse and betrayal to quicken it, just
and natural as it undoubtedly was. And
the will, the embodiment of the writer's
wishes as they had been till that rude and
late awakening, had proved, frail scrap
of paper as it was, a barrier to all his
repentance.

Not for one instant did John West repent
of his own steadfastness in respecting that
barrier. If no other living person than
himself had at that moment been cognizant
of the will's existence, he would have

hastened to place it in proper custody. Yet it was hard to answer his old friend, dashing every hope.

'Do you not know,' he said at last, 'that my cousin has—had, I should say—full power to dispose of the property as he liked ?'

'Bless my heart!' ejaculated the rector, 'but he couldn't leave it out of the family, and there is no one but yourself. That old mother, to be sure. Oh, preposterous!'

'Dear Holbrooke, I know that your feeling for me as a landless man, a penniless waif, has been full as tender as for the heir or the young squire. That consoles me, for, make up your mind to it, once and for all I have ceased to be owner of Swardham. It was a wrench, but it is over, and I accept its consequence as irrevocable. There *is* a will, and I inherit nothing under it.'

He pronounced these words, fatal to his friend's new-born hopes, in no lugubrious tone. The cold fresh air had refreshed and revived him, seeming the more delicious from his late deprivation of it, and his long watches in a close sick-room.

John West was himself again, ay, and a better, happier man than his old self of the prosperous days. He had that within him which could comfort and sustain him in all struggles to come, a better cordial than gold and lands, pride of place, and worldly ambition ; and this his newly-assured love, all the more precious that he had long cherished it in mistaken hopelessness, he must not withhold from Mary's father.

'He has not left it to charities; no—
mortmain—he couldn't,' cried the rector,
almost choking. 'Who, in the name
of—'

'I gained what knowledge I have of the
will in such a way that even to *you* I ought
not to reveal its purport. You will soon
know all about it. Meanwhile, here we are
at your garden wicket, and I—more shame
to me—no better off, no nearer to winning
an honest competence, than when we last
passed it together. Well, I was sore then,
and headstrong, and chock-full of unwarrant-
able squire-like pride that made me morbid
about taking a helping hand, and wrong-
headed about the way to set to work. I'm
no richer yet, but I'm cured of my morose
folly, rector; I'm not above doing anything

for an honest livelihood, and thanking any one kindly who helps me to it.'

By this time they were in the porch, and as the rector, greatly amazed at this cheerfulness under a fresh disappointment, was fumbling for the latch, John West put his two hands on his old friend's shoulders and said softly,—

'What do you think has wrought this change in me? For whose sake am I emboldened to forget all else and make a brave fight, instead of shirking and lurking as I have done?'

The rector murmured inarticulately, cheered vaguely by the other's evident insensibility to Fortune's frowns. He was full of sympathy, but how was he to know who had given John West new courage?

He opened his door and motioned to his companion to enter in front of him.

'Nay; I don't cross your threshold till I have told you the great secret that is my charm against misery and incentive to toil for the future. Rector, I love your Mary, and she loves me. I will never rest till I earn enough to maintain her as my wife.'

'God bless my soul!' said the rector, in a key how unlike that of his last similar ejaculation. 'Mary, my little girl, going to be Mrs. West, *your* wife! Why, my *dear* John—'

'I know I am a shockingly bad match as well as a good many years her senior,' John put in with a rueful smile.

'Bad match! The greatest honour that

could befall my girl or me, only it astounds
me how you came to think of that child, or
when or where ; but come in, come into the
study.'

Ah, that study ! memorable room ! any
other *téte-à-téte* within its walls was as yet
a desecration.

'Why, my dear father-in-law that is to
be, if you and I are to sleep at all before
broad daylight, we had better postpone our
chat till to-morrow.   Do you know it is
four o'clock ?   I have been selfish in dis-
turbing you with my confession to-night ;
but it would out as soon as we got outside
the house where poor Adolphus lies dead (I
mean no disrespect to him, poor fellow, if
I cannot forget my own consolation), and I
hope you will sleep none the worse for my

unbosoming.   To-morrow, or rather at a more seasonable hour of to-day, you shall hear as much of my adventures as you like.'

Sound and untroubled were John West's slumbers that night beneath the roof-tree which sheltered his lady-love. Yet he had within a few hours finally refused to accept from the last male of the race those acres and appanages of the Wests of which he had been reared undisputed heir, which he had for two years enjoyed as his own, which he had ceded with promptitude indeed, but with untold anguish, to their legal owner.

Swardham was dear to him as ever, but honour was now and ever dearer; nor for the most priceless earthly inheritance would he live with a cloud upon that honour's brightness, with the damning consciousness that a whisper had ever gone forth that his fair possession had been questionably won.

CHAPTER IX.

THE PROVISIONAL WILL.

THE body of Adolphus West was laid in the family vault under the chancel of Swardham church with all the pageantry, ugly, unmeaning, and expensive, on which funereal reporters are wont to dilate in their most glowing or stilted phraseology. Of all the useless pomp that ever (dis)graced semi-public obsequies nothing was bated.

'The arrangements reflected the highest credit on our well-known Longborough firm, who need certainly fear no comparison with

the most eminent undertakers of the me-
tropolis.'

So said the *Longborough Gazette* and
the tradesmen of the borough to a man
endorsed the *Gazette's* opinion, considering
that nothing in the life of the last West of
Swardham became him as his leaving its
scene in three handsome coffins, amid in-
describable bedizenment of feathers, hat-
bands, cloaks, and gloves, escorted by an
army of professional man and horse, and
sentinelled by fat black personages who
leaned on black broom-sticks, which had their
own head-gear of voluminous new crape.

As usually happens in such cases, both
before and since Jonas Chuzzlewit gave *carte-
blanche* to Mr. Mould, the trappings were
in an inverse ratio to the regrets of those

who bespoke them for the poor disfigured corpse.

When the prudent Mr. Clark examined in private the last will and testament of his deceased patron, he found in that brief but perfectly valid document no directions as to the testator's burial, no provision, modest or lavish, for the post-mortem expenses.

Under these circumstances Mr. Clark was justified in doing what he was in truth itching to do. He at once, on the day after the death, chartered a fly and drove out to Beausite.

'Well, well,' thought Mr. Clark, as he jolted up the neglected drive and neared the black-streaked and melancholy front of the mansion, 'money is sadly wanted here, no doubt; as well as the supervision of some thoroughly competent business man.'

The earl was at home, so he learned from a yawning and slatternly woman, who opened the great clanking doors under the classic portico; and my lady was also at home, but she had been very sadly for some time, and would see no one. Mr. Clark was content to see the earl in the first instance, and was left by the solitary retainer in the great chilly hall while the earl's pleasure was ascertained, with not so much as a chair to sit down on.

Just as he was waxing somewhat indignant, quite tired of trying to make out what the paintings of the dome had represented before a third of their surface had become obscured or peeled off, he heard a lively whistling, and beheld Lord Fitz-Raymond, who strolled leisurely in with his hands in his shooting-jacket pockets, and perched himself easily on a corner of a great marble slab.

'If it's money you're after, Mr. Clark,' he said carelessly, 'you might as well have stayed in Longborough, and saved your client the fly-hire.'

'My lord! it is money indeed, and money's worth to an extent you little dream of, which is the cause of my opening communications with your lordship's family.'

The earl merely raising his eyebrows and occupying himself with getting a cigarette in working order, Mr. Clark went on in a tone of offended solemnity, due to the weight of his tidings and the scanty courtesy of his reception.

'I am, as you are perhaps aware, the legal representative of the late Mr. West of Swardham ; and it devolves on me to acquaint your lordship and your lordship's sister with that gentleman's testamentary dispositions, and to request certain directions which are immediately necessary.'

Seeing that his auditor was looking first very blank, then puzzled and attentive, Mr. Clark proceeded, in stately language, to un-fold his news, and put Lord FitzRaymond in possession of the purport of the will.

Cool and calm as the young peer had ever shown himself in the many transactions, mainly to his disadvantage, of his career, he was fairly staggered by what he heard.

The cigarette fell unheeded from his lips; he stared in bewilderment at the attorney, still sitting on the slab, and mechanically swinging one leg to and fro. At last he broke out, in vehement excitement,—

'Good God, man! put it in three plain words: am I to understand that Adolphus West makes my sister heiress to Swardham and all he owned besides?'

Disdaining the three words conceded to him, Mr. Clark nodded a nod that was almost a bow.

'But can he? could he? is it legal? will it hold water?'

'My lord, the will by which her ladyship takes the whole property is, though short and informal, a perfectly good will, duly attested, its provisions feasible.'

'What is the date of the will?' sharply inquired the earl.

'It bears date, I fancy, August 26th or 27th last, I am not at this moment prepared to state which.'

'Ah!' a prolonged ah, which ended in a sharp whistle, 'that accounts. You are sure he didn't make another—just before he died, you know?'

'My lord, I am positive that my late client made no other will.'

'Then, Halleluia!' said the earl, and kicked both legs high in air. Instantly resuming his impassive manner after this outburst, he jumped from his seat. 'I will save you the trouble of seeing Lady Georgiana FitzRaymond, Mr. Clark. She is not very well—scarcely up to admitting a stranger; and the news will come best from me. Thank you for the trouble you have been at. Good morning.

Secretly thrilling with disgust at his shabby treatment by an insolent aristocrat, Mr. Clark sent after the earl (who had begun his retreat) such a resonant 'my lord!' that he paused irresolute.

' I come, as I hinted, not only to acquaint her ladyship with important tidings, but to obtain her directions for the obsequies of my deceased client, who omitted the usual or indeed any provisions on that head. As one who will be accountable, I can give no orders till I have her ladyship's sanction for expenditure on such scale as she may consider appropriate.'

The earl whistled again.

'Here's a pretty go ; this is possession with a vengeance, before the poor chap is fairly cold. Why, of course, you may spend what you like ; do the thing properly, by all means.'

Again he tried, ungratefulest of mortals, to get rid of his visitor.

But Mr. Clark proved obstinate, coldly declining to take the earl's permission, and before he left the house obtained an interview with the lady, in whom he saw a future valuable client, better, by reason of her sex, than the late squire, who (as we hnow) had not always been amenable.

When he finally departed he carried a full indemnity for any expenses to be incurred in burying the remains of Adolphus West. And being a Longborough man born

and bred, and not indifferent to popularity
where it could be obtained without private
outlay, he so interpreted the behest, ' to do
the thing properly,' that the funeral and all
its adjuncts were such as have been described, a miracle of costly pomp, a pre-
cedent fondly quoted for years by the
undertakers, silk-mercers, and job masters
of Longborough.

After the ceremony, those who listed of
the followers were bidden by Mr. Clark to
return to the Hall, where the will would be
read. Out of respect to the name he bore,
some dozen of Longshire gentry had attended
the body of the last West of Swardham to
its resting-place. Others had contented
themselves with sending their carriages.

It was a short journey from the Hall to

the Church, and though the least direct route was chosen for greater display of the dismal splendours, no one's horses would be the worse. Of the tenantry more ' followed ' than might have been expected from their grievances and depressed condition.

Poor fellows! they had heard of such things as a year's rent returned by will to each of the testator's tenants. They expected, moreover, with greater confidence to see 'the young Squire,' as they still called John West, which would be a sight for sore eyes, and all the more salutary if it were true, as rumoured, that he was now to be reinstated in the old Hall, and to continue the long line of Squires. The sturdy farmers, some of them bent with age, some in their ruddy prime, clustered near the

service-door of the dining-room, far from
the spot where Mr. Clark sat with a tin
box before him.

Neither John West, who had been chief
mourner, nor the rector of Swardham, was
present. There were three or four gentlemen seated to right and left of the attorney, whom curiosity or friendly interest
in John West had attracted to hear the
will read. And, to the surprise of all,
there was Lord FitzRaymond, who had
both been in the church, and was now
ensconced on a window-seat, where he
busied himself in divesting his hat of the
yards of silk, enough to make a tidy frock
for a child, in which an obsequious man
had that morning swaddled it.

To this audience Mr. Clark took up his

parable. The will which he held (he told them) was the undoubted sole testament of the late Mr. West, though its execution and existence had been unknown, till after that gentleman's death, to his legal adviser. It bore date August 26th, of the year previous, and appeared to have been signed, sealed, and executed at Liverpool, where the two attesting witnesses were still waiters at the hotel in which Mr. West was then staying prior to his unfortunate trip to Norway.

'You will note, gentlemen,' said Mr. Clark, 'that the will is a surprise to me personally, but also (with a side-glance at the window-seat) that the circumstances preclude any allegations of undue influence or lack of testamentary capacity. Gentlemen, it was the expression of **the** deepest sentiments of my late client's heart, sentiments which, although a premature decease forbade their consummation, have taken abiding and solid shape, such shape, gentlemen, as will do all that worldly **abundance** can do to compensate the beneficiary for a doubtless irreparable loss.'

The farmers looked stolidly anxious, the gentry dubious; only the earl, having restored his hat to its normal form, **preserved** his usual aspect **of cool** serenity.

The preamble thus accomplished, **Mr.** Clark unfolded a small and shabby paper, **the very** paper which he had taken from its dead writer's breast. A paltry-looking instrument, yet **by it** Adolphus West **of** Swardham did give **and** bequeath to Georgiana,

daughter of the second and only sister of
the third Earl FitzRaymond, all property,
whether real or personal, of which he should
at his death be possessed. All the broad
corn lands and pastures (whereof the occu-
pants and tillers heard dolorously the trans-
fer), the snug farm-houses with their barns
and straw-yards, the woods, coverts, pre-
serves, orchards, the ancient mansion-house
with its contents, even to the family por-
traits and the old plate; the advowsons,
with next and perpetual right of present-
ation to the rectory of Swardham, and
one or two smaller benefices, the monies
at the bank, or invested in stocks, shares,
or otherwise—all these passed by that
poor sheet of paper to a stranger in blood;
a Longshire woman indeed, but an alien

to the county and the traditions of its ancient houses.

Brief as was the document, it contained something more than the mere bequest. Adolphus West, who had soothed his sick longings for his enchantress, during his wait at Liverpool, by drawing up this will, had begun it in the old-fashioned style, which sets forth the testator's soundness of mind and body, and had added a clause as follows : 'Being about to undertake a voyage, and considering the many perils of such undertakings, I desire so to dispose of my possessions as, in the case of accident, to secure them to that person, who, if my life is spared, will share it and them—and whom, in case this provisional will should take effect, I request to accept all that it conveys in token of my unspeakable love and affection.'

Then followed the bequest, couched in terms so plain and simple as to defy the litigious. Not a legacy, not so much as a few guineas to a servant; no appointment of trustees. Mr. Clark was named co-executor with Lady Georgiana, but took nothing for his trouble. It was plain that there had been no room in the dead man's breast for a thought of any other creature than the one who had enslaved him, while giving him such slight encouragement.

A dead silence fell on the room as the attorney ended these few lines fraught with startling import. The farmers were the first to make a move; all crest-fallen and woe-be-gone, their hopes dashed and their senses dazed, they shuffled out, speechless before the quality, through the door leading to the offices. They had no special know-ledge of the lady whose tenants they so unexpectedly found themselves, but they had 'heard talk' of the 'doings' at Beausite, and their hearts sank within them.

A wistful glance or two some stole at the Earl, but there was nothing in his fresh, handsome face from which any auguries could be drawn. He was looking imperturbably at nothing in particular ; *he* was not mentioned in the will—why should they seek speech of the likes of him ?—what had they to expect from such an one ? So out hurried the farmers, to loose their tongues as they sought their horses, or tramped in knots of three or four down the avenue.

The gentlemen who sat by Mr. Clark were also tongue-tied. They all considered Lord FitzRaymond an immoral man, and a blot on his order, but they had known and respected his father, and felt neither right to utter their deep discontent, nor desire to wound the feelings even of a scamp. As to his sister, to whom this windfall had come, they were still doubtful if she were wife, widow, or divorced woman, and prudently concluded that in her case 'the least said would be the soonest mended.' And so, though the thought of John West was present to them all, none spoke his name, or volunteered an opinion on his cousin's treatment of him.

'Had not the testator a mother living?' asked old Mr. Norton at last.

'Sir, he has,' Mr. Clark answered politely, 'who is otherwise sufficiently provided for.'

In fact, after his mother's departure in wrath and dudgeon from his house, Adolphus had insisted on buying an annuity, whereby her allowance of five hundred a year was secured to his parent in the manner least irksome to him. There were some of the thousands to the fore which John West had surrendered to cover arrears, and in his anger he desired, by one transaction, to settle all scores with the declared enemy of his darling project.

'Ah! indeed,' said old Norton drily. 'Gentlemen, I think we had best get out of this.'

No one had spoken to the Earl as yet. He was, since his boyhood, a stranger to

the Longshire families, whom he had since
his residence at Beausite done nothing to
conciliate.

As Mr. Norton spoke, however, he stepped
from his window seat, and bowed, not
without dignity, to the men who were
rising from their chairs. There was not a
man who could bring himself to address a
word of congratulation to this bad son and
worse landlord on his sister's accession to
fortune, but his graceful coolness made
them uneasy. All made some awkward
movement in return of the Earl's salutation ;
some muttered a 'How-do' or 'Good-bye'
in manifest confusion, and then with a sense
of cutting a sheepish and shame-faced figure
where it behoved them to exhibit im-
pressive severity, they also left the room,

in little better order than the farmers, to spread the unwelcome news each in his own district.

Soon they were driving away, across the park ('There won't be a tree in it soon, I suppose!' said old Norton), and past the churchyard, where masons were closing the vault of the Wests' for the last time. None noticed a young man who was leading a cloaked female to a shabby taxed cart waiting at the lych-gate. Yet there was something unique in that girl in her black frock. She alone of all the numerous attendants at that day's ceremony had shed, was still shedding, tears for the dead man.

'How can you make such a fool of your-self, Sally?' said the young man as he pushed her up into the gig. 'He was as bad to you, as bad could be. Worse than to the rest of us.'

'I know I am a fool, Harry,' sobbed the young woman, 'and you have been very good to humour my folly. But I'd have walked if you hadn't driv me—and oh! I'm thinking of the time he wasn't bad at all.'

Harry Soole growled as he took the reins, but said nothing more to cross his sister. He was thinking that after to-day Sally would surely be herself again, and no longer refuse to look at a rising young grocer who had lately been very attentive to her; and hoping at the same time that a certain young person might be as faithful to himself as his sister had been to her traitorous first love.

'Though it's the blackguards they are fondest of, bless their silly hearts!' thought honest Harry, with his sister beside him, still sniffing behind her veil.

'Of all fossil antediluvians, these Long-shire squires are the most terrible specimens' —so opined Lord FitzRaymond, a trifle nettled for all his unruffled exterior.

He was driving himself home to Beausite, and had Captain Clancy beside him, who had eschewed the funeral as 'not in his line,' and spent the morning between the Hall stables and the village public. He did not know very well what 'fossil ante-diluvians' might be, but chimed in with, 'A duffin lot of screws some of the old buffers had tooled over.'

'But you'll soon wake 'em up in horse-

flesh and other matters, eh, my boy?
Rattlin' good loose boxes there are yonder,
and, by Jove, you're the lad to fill them.'

'Good Lord, Clancy, what a fool you are!
Do you imagine that my sister or I intend
settling down to rot among these rusty
stagers, with their stiff-necked old wives,
and loutish sons, and yea-nay girls? Not
for ten thousand a year and cock-shooting!
Not for Joe!—don't think it, convenient as
you might find it. Neither of us would
have ever come near the place, only for
being so devilish hard-up; and she is as
sick of it as I am. When matters are
arranged we shall both be off fast enough,
you'll find. And in the mean time, don't
talk rot!'

Captain Clancy glanced sidelong out of

his little blood-shot eyes, marvelling what had 'riled' his patron in this lucky dawn of splendid fortune. Beausite had been an uncommonly useful and pleasant resort to him for a long while. The haphazard and irregular style of the place just suited his ideas, and it would be hard to resign these advantages. 'He was never so rough on a fellow, while he was down on his own luck,' he thought in silence; 'wouldn't I be cock-a-whoop and jolly if I had got out of the hole he was in!'

Relenting, as was his way, before the meekness of his friend, the Earl soon said:

'Here, have a weed, old chap!' and, as they puffed in concert, further remarked that 'women are rummy creatures.'

Clancy assenting to this, as he assented

to everything propounded by the peer, he went on meditatively—

'My sister has less nonsense about her than most. In fact, if any woman can be called a real brick, she is the woman. And yet! you'll hardly believe the bother I have had with even her. I suppose she is at this moment the luckiest girl in Great Britain, coming into such a pot of money without having to take to any fellow in the bargain. I didn't really wonder at her shying a bit, when it was a question of running in double harness with the late lamented, who was hardly the sort she had been used to. But here she is, free and rich for life—rid of Aylmer in the nick of time too, and yet she could do nothing but shudder and shake for hours after Clark had gone away ! If it hadn't been for me, and the frightful mess she knew me to be in, I'm hanged if she wasn't capable of chucking the whole thing up—what do you think of that now ?—instead of blessing her lucky stars.'

Captain Clancy, delighted at being restored to favour, was not chary of expressing his sense of Lady G.'s further luck in having a protector with a head on his shoulders, and opined, moreover, that the waywardness of the sex extended even to quadrupeds.

'Look at Tea-gown ! She couldn't have let us all in as she did, if she'd been a he-male.'

This subject once started, the pair 'talked horsy' for the remainder of their drive, and the Earl even made a vague half promise that, if matters went as he hoped, he might do something, on his henchman's behalf, towards 'pulling him through after the Lincoln handicap, if the mare cut up the regular wretch they all expected.'

'Though, mind you,' he added with much solemnity, 'I dare say that it's on the cards that she may be in the running after all, *now*, though it was past all hope while I was in such a beastly fix over the thing. It never rains, you know, but it pours. I dare say she will be in the betting again by the end of the week.'

'Then, please the pigs,' elegantly put in the Captain, 'I'll hedge by the end of a fortnight.'

CHAPTER X.

'OF SWARDHAM STILL.'

IT was a month or more since Adolphus
West's funeral, but the lapse of thrice
nine days had not caused the wonder
to subside with which his will had thrilled
all Longshire. There had been many
rumours afloat of the usual mythical character, each in its turn eagerly discussed
and dropped for another distortion of
facts.

The will was to be disputed! There was
an old entail by which John West was

bound to succeed in spite of a dozen wills!
There was to be a compromise, arranged by
the good offices of the rector of Swardham!
The rector had resigned his benefice in
disgust! John West was about to be tried
for kidnapping a Scotch heiress, and afterwards murdering her! He was going to
take orders in the curacy of Swardham
parish! He had vowed never to see the
place again! Lady Georgiana's husband
had turned up and was to be bought off!
She was about, on the contrary, to contract
a second marriage with a wealthy peer!
She was gone melancholy mad—mad with
joy! The Earl's debts were to be paid
in full—not a farthing was to reach the
Earl's creditors! Thus through every note
of the gamut 'the shrewd pest' rumour

ran without let or abatement, while the gossips and scandal-mongers enjoyed life with unwonted zest.

The chief actors in the drama were meanwhile provokingly indifferent to the public appetite for news. Beausite was shut up, cleared of the 'crew' who had harboured in it, and no one but Mr. Clark knew whither the FitzRaymonds had retired. And as to the rectory folk, they kept themselves to themselves most reprehensibly.

Certain it was that Mr. Auchmuty and some of the elders of the Clan Fife had been in the land, breathing threats against Mr. Holbrooke's guest ; but they had departed, apparently appeased, without taking any one in particular into their confidence. Sir Tancred Woollett could, had he chosen, have told how the matter ended, but the worthy magistrate was not in the habit of indulging the sensation lovers, and justly considered that his wife's relations would be best pleased by his casting a veil over their injurious sus- picions. The amiable Auchmuty indeed had professed himself ill-satisfied with John West's statement, made as it was on oath, but his propensity for making himself ob- jectionable, and proving his brother-in-law's good opinion to be valueless, was oppor- tunely baulked by tidings from the far north.

It transpired that the body of a female had been found by some fishermen, en- tangled in their drag net, off the coast of Inverness, and quietly buried, in order that the finders might keep certain valuables, which had been on the body. A quarrel had, however, arisen as to sharing the spoil, and, after five months, the articles had, through the police, reached the kinsmen of Hilda Fife, and been recognized as her property.

Even after this discovery Mr. Auchmuty would have liked to test the correctness of his estimate of John West's cranial developments by bringing him to a fair trial, but he found himself deserted by the Fifes, who were, after all, Hilda's kith and kin, while he was but a connection, and so gave up the project, grumbling sorely.

The matter had at least one issue, not contemplated by Mr. Auchmuty. Sir Tancred

was deeply moved, and began to cast about
how he could, with the aid of his neighbours, do something substantial for a man
whom he believed the most ill-used by
unjust fate of all men on the earth. He
bore no malice because his good offices had
once been put aside by John West, and
now took earnest counsel with some of the
neighbouring gentry how they might best
testify their unalterable good will. The good
old baronet was delighted to discover in
due course that his friend had found consolation in Mary Holbrooke's love.

'Confound the fellow!' he exclaimed; 'he
can't say us nay if we get up a wedding-
present; and it shall be something worthy
of the county to give, and of Jack West to
receive.

Full of his design, and rejoiced by the heartiness of some of the neighbours whom he canvassed, he at last approached the rector, and took him into his confidence. And then he was met by the astounding intelligence that the rector himself, his daughter, and her husband had decided, immediately after the marriage, on emigrating—going off, bag and baggage, to begin life anew in Australia! It was vain for Sir Tancred, to whom the very notion was horrible, to combat this resolution. The rector quite laughed at him when he pathetically pictured the hardships of a land peopled with convicts and destitute of all resources of civilization.

'It's not half as bad as you make out, Sir Tancred; if it were, how wrong of you to encourage our labourers to go out !'

'Ah, Holbrooke! you were always a sanguine man ; as if you and he could put up with what may suit labouring men ! And if you are mad enough to resign your living (I don't think the bishop could let you hold it if you reside in Australia), what have you left, or what has he ? Capital, my friend ! capital ! that's the one essential for higher class emigrants, and you have none among you.'

' Well, even in that respect we are less short than you fancy. My girl and I can muster a few thousands.'

' Good Heavens ! Holbrooke, I implore you not to be so rash ! Settle it, settle every penny on her ; she may live to want it, poor

dear girl. There's a trifle got or promised,
a sort of wedding present I had hoped to
make it to the young people—but it won't
go far enough, nothing like.'

'My dear old friend, I thank you with
all my heart for this, but you know Jack!
Altered as he is by adversity, with the gold
of his noble character refined by the fire, I
don't think he would like to be set up in
that fashion in his new home; but, listen!
he is not to enter into the partnership
quite empty-handed. Did you not see
by the papers that Frederick Woodvil is
dead?'

'Fred Woodvil! yes. But, alive or dead,
what profit can that selfish old scamp be to
his nephew? Why, I know for a fact that
he sank all he had in an annuity years ago,

and you're not going to tell me that he saved money and has left it to any one who needs it ? '

' What he left behind him would have seemed a mere trifle to Jack in the old days—would not have paid an election bill, I don't doubt—but, such as it is, it is the timeliest help; the most heartening aid to the poor dear fellow, who is buckling to his work nobly, and from my heart I thank God for it.'

Frederick Woodvil was the only brother of Jack's long dead father. He had inherited and squandered a moderate fortune, equal to that similarly dispersed by his brother. But, unlike his brother, he had never married, and he had an income arising from a post in the Treasury.

Long years ago John West could remember his uncle as an occasional guest at
Swardham in the autumn, but Mr. Woodvil
ceased to care for sport when he arrived at
fifty, and professed a general distaste for
relations and the country.

For the last twenty years he had been
living a selfish solitary life in London
lodgings, caring only to resort to his clubs,
where he was known as a brilliant whist-
player, creeping away to Cheltenham or Aix
for a month when London was at its
emptiest, and living, as Sir Tancred said,
on an annuity, bought when he was paid
off at his office, and eked out by the
winnings of the card-table. He had probably long forgotten that he had a blood
relation in the world, and would certainly

not have crossed the street to rescue a hundred nephews from perdition.

Thus it had indeed been a genuine surprise to John West, when Mr. Scott from Longborough presented himself one morning in the first week of February at the rectory, and informed him that he had better take out letters of administration forthwith, as his uncle was dead, intestate, and he was the next of kin.

'Why, there can be nothing but his clothes,' said the heir; 'he didn't even, as far as I know, own a chair or a table.'

'True enough,' said Mr. Scott, with a smile, 'but he owned a share in the London and Bloomsbury Banking Company, and it ought to fetch fifteen hundred pounds if a penny, which is a nice little nest egg, sir!

and I make bold to say I'm uncommonly glad that it has fallen into such good hands. There is money in the bank too, but there may be a few claims against the estate— nothing much though ; you never saw anything so orderly as his papers, and he seems to have kept strict accounts, though he never thought of making a will.'

It was even so. Fifteen years previously the London and Bloomsbury had been a new and struggling concern, and Mr. Frederick Woodvil had grumbled fearfully at accepting from a dabbler in such enterprises this share, in lieu of his winnings at whist at the end of one especially fortunate week. He had finally taken it because he thought he might otherwise get nothing, and he had refused to allow his acquaintance to redeem it subsequently, because he was of an unaccommodating disposition.

Then year by year it had become more valuable, while its owner hesitated as to selling, till the day came on which Frederick Woodvil had to leave it, and all other concerns of earth, and passed to his account. John West's eyes beamed as he shook hands with Mr. Scott.

'To think that I should owe a good turn to Uncle Fred!' he said; 'I suppose it's nonsense to say I am obliged to him, but I am infinitely obliged to you. Fifteen hundred will go a good way in sheep.'

'Sheep, Mr. John! why you don't mean to rent grass-lands hereabouts!'

And then Mr. Scott heard the great news

that John West and certain others, near or
dear to him, were speedily to start for New
South Wales.   It had been the rector's idea
—or inspiration, as Jack would have it.
He had given much thought to the affairs
of his ruined parishioners, the Everetts, and
heard many fair accounts of the great island
from the London agents for the colony.
And when his much-loved pupil talked of
beginning life again in a merchant's office,
and working his way up to a salary on
which he could marry Mary, Holbrooke
burst out suddenly:

'No, my boy, a thousand times no! It
would be the death of you, and of me to
know it of you. Better be a squatter in
the Australian bush than be pent in the
city among people as unlike you as darkness

to light. What say you to our organizing a trip to the antipodes?'

Jack has always declared that his answer and his frame of mind were counterparts of those of Mr. Wilkins Micawber, when that buoyant hero was invited to consider a like proposition. At any rate he took to the idea at once, with a renewal of the energy and vigorous resolution of old days.

When he clearly saw that the rector was yearning to resign his benefice, and accompany those he loved across the wide main, he could urge none of Sir Tancred's prudent cautions, being simply overjoyed at the prospect.

'Now,' he said, 'I can marry Mary off-hand with a clear conscience. I never could have thought of you alone here without a sense of guilt.'

'And I never could have endured my life, in the deserted shell of the old home, with a parish peopled with strangers, and God only knows who at the Hall—but, as it is, what with Mary and you and the Everetts, I can't feel that I shall be altogether running away from my duties. Wherever you may be, you will make up a congregation for the old parson, who won't let you forget old ways.'

'God bless you for it, sir,' Jack said, moved at the picture called up by these words; 'your presence and your ministrations will bring us His blessing, if anything can secure it.'

The only flaw in West's happiness was

his penniless plight. In vain did the rector expatiate on the immense value of such a working-partner, and the absurdity of any-one's expecting such services to be super-added to a contribution of capital.

'I will indeed work my hardest from this hour,' the younger man said, 'but I can never be anything but your steward.'

'Not even my son-in-law ?" retorted the rector grinning ; 'and between near rela-tions what nonsense to apportion the common stock in such fashion.'

On receipt of Frederick Woodvil's leav-ings, however, this last cloud vanished from Jack's horizon, and he could devote himself with fresh ardour to his preparations for his new life (necessitating much running up to town), and to his love-making ; which latter,

Mary Holbrooke vowed, was a very inferior matter, and relegated to mere odd half-hours.

How delightful it was to the lover to rush back to Mary!—how sweet was the meeting!—how charming was the girl's brimming fun, later on, when, for the first time in his life, John West found himself chaffed, and enjoying it; and pretended to growl about familiarity and contempt.

'I was a prig, Mary, in the old days. Yes! I know myself now for a solemn, stiff-backed prig (who collapsed into utter craven feebleness when he lost his padding and had to get off his high horse), and then you used to be respectful—whereas now!'

'Whereas now I am enjoying a short spell of freedom before undertaking to

honour and **obey** a gentleman who gives
himself such an indifferent character. Are
you quite sure there is no danger in accepting the uncle's money?'

'Ah Mary! that invaluable money, for
which I sing a daily *Te Deum !*—who could
have thought it within the compass of those
few poor hundreds to give such pleasure?—
why one might *once* have spent them on a
horse or a picture, and been profoundly
dissatisfied! Seriously, my **pet, I** know
you, who have quickened me to real life,
have brought me luck also. Fortune could
not spite the man whom Mary was good
enough to prefer, and hence this gift from
the unlikeliest of quarters. Poor old uncle
Fred! I wish **it could do** him some good
to have made me so **happy.'**

It was settled that John West and Mary
Holbrooke were to be married at Swardham
early in April, and were to spend the next
week in London, occupying themselves in
final preparations in lieu of a nuptial tour,
and that the rector was then to join them,
with the Everett family in the offing.
By which time they would all be ready
to embark on board a vessel bound for
Sydney.

Meanwhile a great impetus was given
to the scheme by the appearance on the
scene of the rector's old friend Mr. Herbert
and his son, all glowing with enthusiasm at
the heroic intentions of the Holbrookes. It
was at first feared that some awkwardness
might attach to the reappearance at Swardham of young Herbert.

Luckily, however, it transpired that the strapping and inflammable colonial youth had indulged in two or three grand passions since Mary had refused him a hearing, and was now about to return to Australia perfectly heartwhole, and eager for resumption of the free life of the bush-squatter. So far indeed from cherishing any jealousy of John West, he conceived a vehement friendship for that gentleman, and pledged himself to do the impossible on his behalf, on condition that he took up a most suitable run, adjacent to his own, somewhere amid the famous Darling Downs.

' But, my dear fellow,' Jack said, who had been struck with young Herbert's command of money, and lavish orders of pedigree rams ; ' you must bear in mind that I have not a five-pound-note where you have a hundred pounds to lay out!'

Herbert declared that the run in question was the very thing for a man of moderate means, and that in short such beginners were always the people who did best. On his further vowing that he should inevitably go to the bad if disappointed of the neighbours on whom his heart was set, Jack was obliged to promise that he would give Woombya Toombya the preference, in choosing a location for himself and his following. Of the dimensions of that following he had little notion when he spoke.

One fine day, however, about a fortnight before the wedding, he found on his return from London an excited group assembled in the rectory garden and awaiting him.

'Surely I heard cheering,' he said to young Herbert, as they drew near the gate ; and as they emerged from the shrubbery they were greeted with loud 'huzzas !' by some dozen young men, all born and bred in Swardham parish, who, clad in their Sunday suits, were rapturously dinting the lawn with their nailed boots, while they waved their hats and cheered more lustily than ever when they saw their 'young squire,' as he was still called in Swardham.

The rector and Mary were at the drawing-room window, and behind them some one who looked like Sir Tancred—and in two minutes Jack was put in possession of the origin of all the hubbub.

'Here he is ! now speak for yourselves, my lads !' the rector shouted, as excited as the yokels. 'Stop your roaring, and speak up.'

Daniel Brown, a big burly fellow with a shrewd face and a twinkling eye, was pushed to the front, on this hint, and delivered himself of a short speech.

'God bless you, sir,' he said, 'and her that's to be your wife; that's what we all say first;—and then we say, you being so happy-like, starting for Australy with your lady and all, we don't think you're the one to refuse us poor chaps, that you've knowed from boys, a bit of a favour.'

The orator paused and fixed his shrewd eye on Jack, who promptly answered:

'It's little I can do, but if what you ask is to be done, consider it done.'

More huzzas broke out at this, and Daniel shouted amid them :

' Well, sir, we want to go with you, the hull lot of us ! We ain't cripples ezackly ; we could do a tidy day's work a-piece, and, as men you must hev out there, why not them as you know, and as would pretty well kill theirselves to serve you ? '

The cheering had died away, and a group of anxious faces were turned upon Jack, who stood perplexed and deeply moved.

' My lads,' he said, ' I shall never forget this—but, even with assisted passages, it would cost more than I have to spend to rig you and ship you out. I wish to heaven it were not so !—it would be almost like moving the old place itself to have your honest faces

round me ; but I must not mislead you, I
fear it is impossible.'

To his surprise the men looked not
unpleased with his answer. They nudged
each other, swaying to and fro, and looked
past Jack into the drawing-room window.
Then the agitated rector pushed Sir Tancred
Woollett to the front, who took up his
parable.

'My dear boy,' he said—'for boy you
are still to me,—I was calling on our friend
here when this deputation arrived. We
took the liberty of tapping them (so to
speak), and discussing their modest proposal.
And it occurred to friend Holbrooke that
the sole difficulty likely to arise—the money
difficulty—was one which, if you choose, I
can have the pleasure of quelling for you in

a trice. I express no opinion on this emigration scheme, because you are all too far gone in it to hearken to wisdom ; but if you must *go*, I should desire you to have a few folks round you who at any rate were never convicts. Look you here then ! Among a few of your old neighbours and friends a sum has been subscribed to buy you and Mistress Molly here a wedding-gift. It is three hundred pounds, and I have luckily been too distracted by your eccentric proceedings to have settled on anything ! You cut all sensible ground from under a man's feet with your ramping off to Australia. I ran over all the usual lists of presents, but I couldn't persuade myself that a silver tea-tray and pair of wine-coolers would be exactly the thing for the bush—so take the

cash and do what you like with it. And if
you like to buy outfits for these strapping
lads, and pay their passages or the balance
of them, why I am empowered to say that
in pleasing yourself you will best please the
subscribers.'

Gratefully pressing the old man's hand,
Jack turned to his sweetheart and asked :

' Mary, what do you say ? This money
was a present for you ; what shall it be ? '

Mary's eyes shone with a ' happy mist '
as she said :

' I choose what you choose, and I think it
will be—*these.*'

She stepped forward, and stretching her
arms wide, lightly touched with her little
hands the cuffs of the foremost brawny
fellows, who were again deafening everybody

with their cheers. She knew them all—
knew them since she and they were mere
brats and urchins, and at this moment she
loved them for their loyalty.

Then she stood thrilling by Jack's side,
while in husky tones he accepted the men's
offer and Sir Tancred's proposal. He could
muster no flowers of speech ; but there was
an eloquence in his features which all who
beheld it comprehended, and his heart was
brim-full of humble gratitude.

'You trust yourselves to me,' he concluded, 'and God so deal with me as I with
you. You leave your old mothers, or fathers,
or homes, to go far away with me—may
I so thrive as I give your parents cause to
say you did well in trusting me ! If I can't
find work at a fair wage for you all at first,

here is one who will — Mr. Herbert, our
next neighbour that is to be, and son of a
gentleman whose helpfulness to me just now
is not to be told in words.'

There was a contented hum and buzz as
Jack's little speech ended. After a minute
Daniel stepped forward again.

' Askin' your pardon, sir, but what might
be the name of the part where we're
going ? '

Jack smiled as he answered :

' The district is known as Darling Downs,
and (set me right, Herbert, if I mull it) I
believe the sheep-run which is to be ours
is called Woombya Toombya.'

Mary and Herbert burst out laughing at
Dan Brown's comically puzzled face.

' I doubt I can't come it, sir, not if I

troubled you to say it again.   But if you'll
excuse a chap like me starting the notion—
why not take and call it after the old parish
here ?   Where you are, sir, and the rector,
and Miss Mary, not to mention we chaps,
there's bound to be Swardham ; and, excuse
me, gentry all, but I'm blowed if this spot
didn't ought to lose the name, if so be that
there can't be no more than one Swardham
at a time.'

Daniel's mates interrupted him by their
loud assent to this position.

' West of Swardham ! all the world over,'
they bawled : ' it an't Swardham without
e'er a West !—and it'll be Swardham right
enough, wheres'ever it be, if you're at the
head of it, squire ! '

The rector was fairly in tears by this

time. He seized his son-in-law's hand and faltered out :

'I add my voice to theirs! Be West of Swardham still. Let a new world give me that happiness which ·I had lost here.'

And what could John West do but consent? He had distressed Mr. Holbrooke by professing himself in doubt as to what his own name really was—a doubt which ill-became a man on the verge of marriage. Born Woodvil, bred West, condemned by circumstances to be Wood for a while, he declared himself rather in favour of the last, as most unassuming and suitable for a sheep-owner in the colonies.

Now he looked into the rector's moist appealing eyes, and felt that the question

was settled for him.   The old familiar name
and style was to be his till death, and,
though he had clung not at all to departed
grandeur, and knew that his life would be
as unlike that of the Squires West as his
dwelling would be unlike the old Hall, he
felt proud of his title, and grateful to those
who had urged his assumption of it.   For
at Swardham, where never more would a
Squire West reign, none knew who would
next bear sway.

The Hall and the broad estates were
already advertised by those famous auc-
tioneers Messrs. Fraser and Fibb.   And it
was not till John West with his wife and
the rector were on the ocean that Longshire
received the new owner in the person of
Samuel Swithinbank, Esq., the well-known

boiler-maker and engineer—a rich man and a reputed Radical.

There followed an auction of the contents of the Hall, for Mrs. Swithinbank, imbued with Italian art-notions, intended to remodel the interior, as she could not persuade her husband to pull the whole pile down. A clearance being thus effected, the lady laid down 'compo' floors, and threw three rooms into one, and generally did away with all comfort or congruity with our English climate. Even then, she so pined for a loggia, that the indulgent Swithinbank, who had fads about his water supply, consented to add two towers to the poor old house, which should conceal vast cisterns in their upper parts, and gratify the lady with a loggia apiece lower down.

This done, she discovered that the alliteration in 'Samuel Swithinbank of Swardham' would be simply deadly, and never rested till the name was changed. 'The Towers, near Longborough,' is now the Swithinbank postal address, and poor little Swardham village is fallen into great obscurity. The new landlord is not a hard man, though he considers (and yearly with greater seriousness) that he paid far too much for the estate; but there are people in Swardham who find his practical good-sense a poor substitute for 'Madam West's' unforgotten tenderness —or 'Miss Mary's' cheerful presence.

Of course there is a new rector! Mr. Holbrooke's resignation did not legally take effect till the sale had been completed, and a cousin of Mrs. Swithinbank is his successor.

He is young and fervid, but his fondness
for an advanced ritual has at present
attracted little sympathy in the parish,
though his vestments and those of his altar
are Mrs. Swithinbank's own gifts, and certainly enough to dazzle the most obstinate
Protestant.

Lady Georgiana FitzRaymond, to the
abiding mortification of Mr. Clark, invested the greater part of the very handsome sum obtained by selling Swardham in
French rentes and other foreign securities.
She has made her home in Paris, where she
has a beautiful Hôtel in the Avenue Villars,
and is a personage of much consideration
in fashionable circles. She would have
been on a still higher pinnacle had the
days of the Empire been prolonged. The

T 2

atmosphere of that Court would have suited her admirably, and with her wealth, beauty, and 'chic' she would have been among its brightest ornaments.

Her brother lives with her, and defies her occasional plots to marry him. Were it not for her desire to spite her step-mother, Lady G. would take no step to give the earl a home of his own, for he is most useful to her, has given up 'plunging,' and spends no more than she can afford to allow him at his 'cercles,' where he is a great authority on racing. He has been steward at Longchamps and Chantilly, has won no end of 'Prix de Jocky-Club,' and finds life not only bearable but pleasant, thanks to an early acquaintance with the French tongue.

Beausite is let, leased, to Lady G.'s disgust, to the Countess Dowager FitzRaymond. Under that gentle lady's auspices all smirch and stain has disappeared, all has been placed in due and decent repair. She and her girls sing their hymns and lead their religious lives, in the rooms where the foreign ladies chattered, capered, and puffed cigars. Her boys coming home from Eton or Cambridge furnish her greatest excitement, her sole connection with the world outside of Longshire.

Sir Tancred writes once a quarter, to his 'exiles' as he calls them still, and shakes his head with a long sigh as his pen traces 'West of Swardham' on the envelope—for he misses old friends—and there is no Swardham this side of the globe!

In that far-away Swardham, in spite of occasional checks by drought, and troubles with 'free selectors,' a moderate degree of prosperity is vouchsafed to the honest exertion, unremitting and often anxious, of John West.

It may be added, however, that whatever his cares as squatter may at times be, he has found none as yet which could lessen his relish for his short restful hours, cheered as they are by the best of wives.

Mr. Holbrooke does great things as parson of a vast though thinly peopled region. Among his parishioners is one of whom he has great hopes, though he has not yet obtained from him a confession of orthodoxy, a teetotal man who works hard on a small run of his own, and is invincibly cheerful under all circumstances, though his pleasant wit sparkles most on the frequent occasions when he is a guest at Swardham. That man's name is Eric Björnsen.

THE END.

Clay and Taylor, Printers, Bungay, Suffolk.

MESSRS. HURST AND BLACKETT'S
LIST OF NEW WORKS.

THE PICTORIAL PRESS: Its Origin and Progress. By Mason Jackson. 1 vol. demy 8vo. With 150 Illustrations. 16s.

THE MEMOIRS OF A CAMBRIDGE CHORISTER. By William Glover. 2 vols. crown 8vo. 21s.

THE LIFE AND ADVENTURES OF PEG WOFFINGTON: With Pictures of the Period in which She Lived. By J. Fitzgerald Molloy, Author of "Court Life Below Stairs," &c. *Second Edition.* 2 vols. crown 8vo. With Portrait. 21s.

"These volumes are very agreeably written. In dealing with the literary and dramatic personages of the period, Mr. Molloy is a faithful chronicler not only in spirit but also as to facts. There is no prominent personage about whom a number of characteristic anecdotes are not told. The author also gives a brilliant sketch of life in the Irish capital half a century before the Union."—*St. James's Gazette.*

"Peg Woffington makes a most interesting central figure, round which Mr. Molloy has made to revolve a varied and picturesque panorama of London life in the middle of the eighteenth century. He sees things in the past so clearly, grasps them so tenaciously, and reproduces them so vividly, that they come to us without any of the dust and rust of time. Horace Walpole, Lord Hervey, Colley Cibber, Dr. Doran, Lord Macaulay, George Anne Bellamy, Macklin, and other authorities, are laid unstintedly under contribution for the biographies which the author narrates and the good stories that he tells; but he has a gift and a charm which are peculiarly his own."—*G. A. S. in Illustrated London News.*

"As a story this life of Peg Woffington is excellent reading. The character of the lively actress is fairly illustrated in those scenes in which she bears a part, whether humorous, sentimental, pathetic, or tragic. Mr. Molloy has filled up the pages intervening between his sketches with anecdotes, and has succeeded in presenting a picture of the stage world in the days of the second George which could not easily be surpassed. Of Kitty Clive, of Garrick, of Macklin, of Foote the witty, and of Johnson the ponderous, many lively stories are told."—*Post.*

A TWO MONTHS' CRUISE IN THE MEDITERRANEAN IN THE STEAM-YACHT "CEYLON." By Surgeon-General Munro, M.D., C.B. Author of "Reminiscences of Military Service with the 93rd Sutherland Highlanders." 1 vol. crown 8vo. 7s. 6d.

"A frank, hearty record of an experience which those who shared it must remember with cordial pleasure."—*Pall Mall Gazette.*

"In this delightful cruise Dr. Munro saw much that was picturesque and interesting. The book will give pleasure to many readers."—*Morning Post.*

"This book is characterised by a simple-minded kindliness of tone which makes it very pleasant reading."—*Graphic.*

"A brisk and pleasing description of what is perhaps as delightful a life as a tourist could spend. The author's narrative partakes of the cheerfulness of the voyage."—*Daily News.*

MESSRS. HURST AND BLACKETT'S
NEW WORKS—*Continued.*

WITHOUT GOD: NEGATIVE SCIENCE AND NATURAL

ETHICS. By PERCY GREG, Author of "The Devil's Advocate,' "Across the Zodiac," &c. 1 vol. demy 8vo. 12s.

"Mr. Greg has condensed much profound thought into his book, and has fully succeeded in maintaining the interest of the discussion throughout."—*Morning Post.*

"This work is ably written; there are in it many passages of no ordinary power and brilliancy. It is eminently suggestive and stimulating."—*Scotsman.*

"This is the work of a man full of thought upon a number of highly important subjects, and of strong convictions strongly enunciated, which no one can read without benefit."—*Morning Advertiser.*

"Mr. Greg's speculative works are always worth study, and this certainly not the least of them. It is a powerful and instructive book for the doubter to read, and the author has given us many discussions of great subtlety and depth."— *Spectator.*

SIBERIAN PICTURES. By LUDWIK NIEMOJOWSKI.

Edited, from the Polish, by MAJOR SZULCZEWSKI. 2 vols 21s.

"This book contains a good deal of interesting matter. M. Niemojowski's description of Siberian game and the hunting of it is clearly valuable, and shows that he really has lived among the people. His work is not without interest to ethnographers, for it deals with almost every race that inhabits Siberia—Tunguzes and Tartars, Samoyedes and Ostiaks, the Buriats of Lake Baikal, and the Gilliacks of the Pacific coasts."—*Saturday Review.*

"Major Szulczewski has done a service by translating from the Polish the interesting account which Mr. Niemojowski has given of the dreary land in which he spent so many years of exile. The book contains a number of very interesting stories."—*Athenæum.*

"This book contains by far the most exhaustive and reliable account which has yet been given in English of Siberia."—*British Quarterly Review.*

REMINISCENCES OF MILITARY SERVICE

WITH THE 93rd SUTHERLAND HIGHLANDERS. By SURGEON-GENERAL MUNRO, M.D., C.B., Formerly Surgeon of the Regiment. 1 vol. demy 8vo. 15s.

"This is a book of interesting recollections of active military campaigning life. It is told in a frank, simple, and unpretentious manner."—*Illustrated London News.*

"This book is not only bright and lively, but thoroughly good-natured. What makes these reminiscences exceptionally readable is the amount of illustrative anecdote with which they are interspersed. The author has a keen appreciation of humour, with the knack of recalling appropriate stories."—*Saturday Review.*

"There is much in these interesting reminiscences that will gratify while it pains the reader. A book like this, which portrays the horrors and not merely the showy side of war, has distinct usefulness. Dr. Munro recounts many incidents with pardonable pride."—*Pall Mall Gazette.*

THE FRIENDSHIPS OF MARY RUSSELL

MITFORD: AS RECORDED IN LETTERS FROM HER LITERARY CORRESPONDENTS. Edited by the REV. A. G. L'ESTRANGE, Editor of "The Life of Mary Russell Mitford," &c. 2 vols. 21s.

"These letters are all written as to one whom the writers love and revere. Miss Barrett is one of Miss Mitford's correspondents, all of whom seem to be inspired with a sense of excellence in the mind they are invoking. Their letters are extremely interesting, and they strike out recollections, opinions, criticisms, which will hold the reader's delighted and serious attention."—*Daily Telegraph.*

"In this singular and probably unique book Miss Mitford is painted, not in letters of her own nor in letters written of her, but in letters addressed to her; and a true idea is thus conveyed of her talent, her disposition, and of the impression she made upon her friends. It seldom happens that anyone, however distinguished, receives such a number of letters well worth reading as were addressed to Miss Mitford; and the letters from her correspondents are not only from interesting persons, but are in themselves interesting."—*St. James's Gazette.*

2

MEMOIRS OF MARSHAL BUGEAUD, FROM HIS PRIVATE CORRESPONDENCE AND ORIGINAL DOCUMENTS, 1784—1849. By the COUNT H. D'IDEVILLE. Edited, from the French, by CHARLOTTE M. YONGE. 2 vols. demy 8vo. 30s.

"Marshal Bugeaud was a grand soldier, a noble-minded, patriotic citizen. His Algerian career was brilliant, eventful, and successful, both as regards military command and civil administration."—*Times.*

"This is a work of great value to the student of French history. A perusal of the book will convince any reader of Bugeaud's energy, his patriotism, his unselfishness, and his philanthropy and humanity. He was, indeed, a general who may serve as a pattern to all countries, and his name deserves to live long in the memory of his countrymen. His sagacious, far-seeing opinions on military as well as civil matters they will do well to ponder and take to heart."—*Athenæum.*

"Miss Yonge has done well to edit for the English public M. d'Ideville's life of the conqueror of Abd-el-Kader. Marshal Bugeaud was worth knowing as a man even more than as a soldier. M. d'Ideville is both an enthusiastic and a veracious chronicler."—*Spectator.*

"Marshal Bugeaud **was** a more remarkable man than nine out of ten who have been the idol of a biographer, and his career is fertile in episodes or incidents characteristic of the times, and throwing light on history."—*Quarterly Review.*

The present biography of Marshal Bugeaud is very interesting, and it is so well translated that it reads like an original work."—*Daily News.*

"Readers will be thankful to Miss Yonge for having brought **so** entertaining and instructive a work under their notice."—*Standard.*

COURT LIFE BELOW STAIRS; or, LONDON UNDER THE FIRST GEORGES, 1714—1760. By J. FITZGERALD MOLLOY. *Second Edition.* Vols. 1 and 2. Crown 8vo. 21s.

"Well written, full of anecdotes, and with its facts admirably grouped, this excellent work will prove of the greatest value to all who desire to know what manner of men the first Electors of Hanover who came here really were. Pictures of Court life so drawn cannot fail to be very instructive. Some of the word pictures are wonderfully well drawn."—*Daily Telegraph.*

VOLS. III. and IV. of COURT LIFE BELOW STAIRS; or, LONDON UNDER THE LAST GEORGES, 1760—1830. By J. FITZGERALD MOLLOY. *Second Edition.* 21s. Completing the Work.

"The reigns of George the Third and George the Fourth are no less interesting and instructive than those of George the First and George the Second. Mr. Molloy's style is bright and fluent, picturesque and animated, and he tells his stories with unquestionable skill and vivacity."—*Athenæum.*

"These last two volumes of Mr. Molloy's 'Court Life Below Stairs' are likely to attain as much popularity as the first two did. The narrative is fluent and amusing, and is far more instructive than nine-tenths of the novels which are published nowadays."—*St. James's Gazette.*

GRIFFIN, AHOY! A Yacht Cruise to the LEVANT, and Wanderings in EGYPT, SYRIA, THE HOLY LAND, GREECE, and ITALY in 1881. By GENERAL E H. MAXWELL, C.B. One vol. demy 8vo. With Illustrations. 15s.

"The cruise of the *Griffin* affords bright and amusing reading from its beginning to its end. General Maxwell writes in a frank and easy style.—*Morning Post.*

WITH THE CONNAUGHT RANGERS IN QUARTERS, CAMP, AND ON LEAVE. By GENERAL E. H. MAXWELL, C.B., Author of "Griffin, Ahoy." 1 vol. 8vo. With Illustrations. 15s.

"A warm welcome may be presaged for General Maxwell's new work. It is an eminently readable book, quite apart from the special attraction it must possess for all who are, or who have been, connected with the gallant 88th."—*Daily Telegraph.*

"When General Maxwell made his *début* in that capital book, 'Griffin, Ahoy!' we expressed a hope that we should soon meet him again. This expectation is now fulfilled, and again we have to congratulate the author on a distinct success. Scarcely a page in his volume but has its little anecdote, and these stories have a real touch of humour in them."—*Globe.*

GLIMPSES OF GREEK LIFE AND SCENERY.

By Agnes Smith, Author of " Eastern Pilgrims," &c. Demy 8vo. With Illustrations and Map of the Author's Route. 15s.

"A truthful picture of the country through which the author travelled. It is naturally and simply told, in an agreeable and animated style. Miss Smith displays an ample acquaintance and sympathy with all the scenes of historic interest, and is able to tell her readers a good deal of the present condition and prospects of the people who inhabit the country."—*St. James's Gazette.*

"Every lover of Greece must hail with pleasure each new book of travels in that country which tends to increase the interest of English people in Greece, and spreads the knowledge that it is not only delightful, but quite safe, to travel there. Miss Smith's 'Glimpses' are lively and pleasant."—*Academy.*

"These 'Glimpses' are presented to us in a very bright and sensible fashion. It is a very agreeable and instructive book. The chapter on the language and character of the modern Greeks is well worth reading for the sound judgment and knowledge of the subject which it displays."—*Pall Mall Gazette.*

LIFE OF MOSCHELES; WITH SELECTIONS FROM HIS DIARIES AND CORRESPONDENCE. By His Wife. 2 vols. large post 8vo. With Portrait. 24s.

"This life of Moscheles will be a valuable book of reference for the musical historian, for the contents extend over a period of threescore years, commencing with 1794, and ending at 1870. Moscheles writes fairly of what is called the 'Music of the Future,' and his judgments on Herr Wagner, Dr. Liszt, Rubenstein, Dr. von Bülow, Litolff, &c., whether as composers or executants, are in a liberal spirit. He recognizes cheerfully the talents of our native artists: Sir S. Bennett, Mr. Macfarren, Madame Goddard, Mr. J. Barnett, Mr. Hullah, Mr. A. Sullivan, &c. The volumes are full of amusing anecdotes."—*Athenæum.*

MONSIEUR GUIZOT IN PRIVATE LIFE (1787-1874). By His Daughter, Madame DE WITT. Translated by Mrs. SIMPSON. 1 vol. demy 8vo. 15s.

"Madame de Witt has done justice to her father's memory in an admirable record of his life. Mrs. Simpson's translation of this singularly interesting book is in accuracy and grace worthy of the original and of the subject."—*Saturday Review.*

WORDS OF HOPE AND COMFORT TO THOSE IN SORROW. Dedicated by Permission to THE QUEEN. *Fourth Edition.* 1 vol. small 4to. 5s.

"The writer of the tenderly-conceived letters in this volume was Mrs. Julius Hare, a sister of Mr. Maurice. They are instinct with the devout submissiveness and fine sympathy which we associate with the name of Maurice; but in her there is added a winningness of tact, and sometimes, too, a directness of language, which we hardly find even in the brother. The letters were privately printed and circulated, and were found to be the source of much comfort, which they cannot fail to afford now to a wide circle. A sweetly-conceived memorial poem, bearing the well-known initials, 'E. H. P.', gives a very faithful outline of the life."—*British Quarterly Review.*

PLAIN SPEAKING. By Author of " John Halifax, Gentleman." 1 vol. crown 8vo. 10s. 6d.

"We recommend 'Plain Speaking' to all who like amusing, wholesome, and instructive reading. The contents of Mrs. Craik's volume are of the most multifarious kind, but all the papers are good and readable, and one at least of them of real importance."—*St. James's Gazette.*

HURST AND BLACKETT'S
SIX-SHILLING NOVELS

WE TWO.
By EDNA LYALL,
Author of "Donovan," &c.

"This book is well-written and full of interest. The story abounds with a good many light touches, and is certainly far from lacking in incident."—*Times.*

"'We Two' contains many very exciting passages and a great deal of information. Miss Lyall is a capable writer of fiction, and also a clear-headed thinker."—*Athenæum.*

"We recommend all novel-readers to read this novel, with the care which such a strong, uncommon, and thoughtful book demands and deserves."—*Spectator.*

"There is artistic realism both in the conception and the delineation of the personages; the action and interest are unflaggingly sustained from first to last, and the book is pervaded by an atmosphere of elevated and earnest thought."—*Scotsman.*

THE BRANDRETHS.
By the Right Hon. A. J. B. BERESFORD HOPE, M.P.,
Author of "Strictly Tied Up."

"In 'The Brandreths' we have a sequel to Mr. Beresford Hope's clever novel of 'Strictly Tied Up,' and we may add that it is a decided improvement on his maiden effort. Mr. Hope writes of political life and the vicissitudes of parties with the knowledge and experience of a veteran politician. The novel is one which will repay careful reading."—*Times.*

"'The Brandreths' has all the charm of its predecessor. The great attraction of the novel is the easy, conversational, knowledgeable tone of it; the sketching from the life, and yet not so close to the life as to be malicious, men, women, periods, and events, to all of which intelligent readers can fit a name."—*Spectator.*

SOPHY:
OR THE ADVENTURES OF A SAVAGE.
By VIOLET FANE,
Author of "Denzil Place," &c.

"'Sophy' is the clever and original work of a clever woman. Its merits are of a strikingly unusual kind. It is charged throughout with the strongest human interest. It is, in a word, a novel that will make its mark."—*World.*

"This novel is as amusing, piquant, droll, and suggestive as it can be. It overflows with humour, nor are there wanting touches of genuine feeling. To considerable imaginative power, the writer joins keen observation."—*Daily News.*

MY LORD AND MY LADY.
By Mrs. FORRESTER,
Author of "Viva," "Mignon," &c.

"This novel will take a high place among the successes of the season. It is as fresh a novel as it is interesting, as attractive as it is realistically true, as full of novelty of presentment as it is of close study and observation of life."—*World.*

"A love story of considerable interest. The novel is full of surprises, and will serve to while away a leisure hour most agreeably."—*Daily Telegraph.*

HIS LITTLE MOTHER: and Other Tales.
By the Author of "John Halifax, Gentleman."

"This is an interesting book, written in a pleasant manner, and full of shrewd observation and kindly feeling. It is a book that will be read with interest, and that cannot be lightly forgotten."—*St. James's Gazette.*

"The Author of 'John Halifax' always writes with grace and feeling, and never more so than in the present volume."—*Morning Post.*

Under the Especial Patronage of Her Majesty.

Published annually, in One Vol., royal 8vo, with the Arms beautifully engraved, handsomely bound, with gilt edges, price 31s. 6d.

LODGE'S PEERAGE
AND BARONETAGE,
CORRECTED BY THE NOBILITY.

THE FIFTY-THIRD EDITION FOR 1884 IS NOW READY.

LODGE'S PEERAGE AND BARONETAGE is acknowledged to be the most complete, as well as the most elegant, work of the kind. As an established and authentic authority on all questions respecting the family histories, honours, and connections of the titled aristocracy, no work has ever stood so high. It is published under the especial patronage of Her Majesty, and is annually corrected throughout, from the personal communications of the Nobility. It is the only work of its class in which, *the type being kept constantly standing*, every correction is made in its proper place to the date of publication, an advantage which gives it supremacy over all its competitors. Independently of its full and authentic information respecting the existing Peers and Baronets of the realm, the most sedulous attention is given in its pages to the collateral branches of the various noble families, and the names of many thousand individuals are introduced, which do not appear in other records of the titled classes. For its authority, correctness, and facility of arrangement, and the beauty of its typography and binding, the work is justly entitled to the place it occupies on the tables of Her Majesty and the Nobility.

LIST OF THE PRINCIPAL CONTENTS.

Historical View of the Peerage.
Parliamentary Roll of the House of Lords.
English, Scotch, and Irish Peers, in their orders of Precedence.
Alphabetical List of Peers of Great Britain and the United Kingdom, holding superior rank in the Scotch or Irish Peerage.
Alphabetical list of Scotch and Irish Peers, holding superior titles in the Peerage of Great Britain and the United Kingdom.
A Collective list of Peers, in their order of Precedence.
Table of Precedency among Men.
Table of Precedency among Women.
The Queen and the Royal Family.
Peers of the Blood Royal.
The Peerage, alphabetically arranged.
Families of such Extinct Peers as have left Widows or Issue.
Alphabetical List of the Surnames of all the Peers.

The Archbishops and Bishops of England and Ireland.
The Baronetage alphabetically arranged.
Alphabetical List of Surnames assumed by members of Noble Families.
Alphabetical List of the Second Titles of Peers, usually borne by their Eldest Sons.
Alphabetical Index to the Daughters of Dukes, Marquises, and Earls, who, having married Commoners, retain the title of Lady before their own Christian and their Husband's Surnames.
Alphabetical Index to the Daughters of Viscounts and Barons, who, having married Commoners, are styled Honourable Mrs. ; and, in case of the husband being a Baronet or Knight, Hon. Lady.
A List of the Orders of Knighthood.
Mottoes alphabetically arranged and translated.

"This work is the most perfect and elaborate record of the living and recently deceased members of the Peerage of the Three Kingdoms as it stands at this day. It is a most useful publication. We are happy to bear testimony to the fact that scrupulous accuracy is a distinguishing feature of this book."—*Times.*

"Lodge's Peerage must supersede all other works of the kind, for two reasons: first, it is on a better plan ; and secondly, it is better executed. We can safely pronounce it to be the readiest, the most useful, and exactest of modern works on the subject."—*Spectator.*

"A work of great value. It is the most faithful record we possess of the aristocracy of the day."—*Post.*

"The best existing, and, we believe, the best possible Peerage. It is the standard authority on the subject. —*Standard.*

THE NEW AND POPULAR NOVELS.
PUBLISHED BY HURST & BLACKETT.

KEEP TROTH. By WALTER L. BICKNELL, M.A.
3 vols.
" There are many passages in this clever and interesting novel which lead to more serious reflection than works of fiction, even of the higher class, are wont to awaken."—*Spectator.*

THE MASTER OF ABERFELDIE. By JAMES GRANT, Author of " The Romance of War," &c. 3 vols.
" The graphic picture of the battle of Tel-el-Kebir, which Mr. Grant gives in his novel, augments the effect of a romance which bears witness to the author's powers."—*St. James's Gazette.*

THE PITY OF IT. By Mrs. M. E. SMITH, Author of " It Might have Been," " Tit for Tat," &c. 3 vols.
" A bright story. The principal character is fresh and lovable. The plot is well worked out in all its details."—*Morning Post.*
" A very readable story. There is plenty of movement and mystery in the latter part of the book."—*Daily Telegraph.*

VENUS' DOVES. By IDA ASHWORTH TAYLOR.
3 vols.
" 'Venus' Doves' is a graceful and well-written novel. Miss Taylor's studies of character are finished and delicate, and the actors are cultivated and refined people. It is a pleasant book."—*Athenæum.*
" A very pretty story, very prettily told. We recommend it strongly as a tale which is interesting as well as pure and good."—*Standard.*

THE MAN SHE CARED FOR. By F. W. ROBINSON, Author of " Grandmother's Money," &c. 3 vols.
" A genuinely pleasant tale. The interest accumulates as the story proceeds. It contains some passages and some delineations of character which may compare with Mr. Robinson's most successful work."—*Athenæum.*

WE TWO. By EDNA LYALL, Author of " Donovan," &c. 3 vols.
" A work of deep thought and much power. Serious as it is, it is now and then brightened by rays of genuine humour. Altogether this story is more and better than a novel."—*Morning Post.*

TO HAVE AND TO HOLD. By SARAH STREDDER, Author of " The Fate of a Year," &c. 3 vols.
" This novel is strong and romantic. It is a tale of real life, with incidents of so stirring a nature that they cannot fail to arrest attention."—*Morning Post.*

OMNIA VANITAS: A TALE OF SOCIETY. By Mrs. FORRESTER, Author of " Viva," &c. *Third Edition.* 1 vol.
" This book is pleasant and well meant. Here and there are some good touches: Sir Ralph is a man worth reading about."—*Academy.*

DONOVAN. By EDNA LYALL, Author of " We Two," &c. 3 vols.
" This novel is thoroughly well written; it is full of scenes which prove the author's powers of observation and description; it contains variety of incident, and has much real merit. The character of Donovan is powerfully drawn."—*Morning Post.*

A BEGGAR ON HORSEBACK. By Mrs. POWER O'DONOGHUE, Author of " Ladies on Horseback," &c. 3 vols.
" This story has a great deal of real pathos, and is interesting as a study of Hibernian character."—*Athenæum.*

THE NEW AND POPULAR NOVELS.
PUBLISHED BY HURST & BLACKETT.

LOVE AND MIRAGE. By M. Betham-Edwards.
Author of "Kitty," "Bridget," &c. 2 vols.

WEST OF SWARDHAM. By the Rev. W. O.
Peile, Author of "Tay." 3 vols.

CYCLAMEN. By Mrs. Randolph. Author of
"Gentianella," "Wild Hyacinth," &c. 3 vols. *(In November.)*

RALPH RAEBURN. By John Berwick Harwood.
Author of "Lady Flavia," &c. 3 vols.

THE DOUBLE DUTCHMAN. By Catharine
Childar, Author of "The Future Marquis," &c. 3 vols.
"This very readable book is above the average of novels of its kind. It deals
brightly with scenes of modern social life."—*Athenæum.*
"This novel is striking, amusing, and full of surprises. The story is graphically
written, and abounds in stirring incident. It is altogether a book that deserves
to be read."—*Post.*

JOY. By May Crommelin, Author of "Queenie,"
"Orange Lily," &c. 3 vols.
"Miss Crommelin has here produced a powerful novel. It is as healthy and
pure as it is strong and original."—*British Quarterly Review.*
"A powerfully written tale. The plot is dramatic and full of human interest.
There is much to commend in this novel."—*Morning Post.*

ON THE SPUR OF THE MOMENT. By John
Mills, Author of "The Old English Gentleman," &c. 3 vols.
"There are many graceful and some pathetic scenes in this book. The chapters
on sport are bright, graphic, and full of movement."—*Morning Post.*

INCOGNITA. By Henry Cresswell, Author of
"A Modern Greek Heroine," &c. 3 vols.
"This novel has in it much to please and satisfy. Most of the characters are
finely drawn, but the heroine is more skilfully described than any of the rest."—
Athenæum.
"A clever, entertaining novel. It distances its predecessors by the same hand
in ability and invention."—*Academy.*

THE COUNTER OF THIS WORLD. By Lilias
Wassermann and Isabella Weddle, Authors of "A Man of the
Day," "David Armstrong," &c. 3 vols.
"A powerfully-written story. Many of the situations possess a strong dramatic
interest. The tale has a wholesome ring about it."—*Globe.*
"This novel is powerfully written, and will repay perusal."—*Post.*

LADY LOWATER'S COMPANION. By the
Author of "St. Olave's," "Janita's Cross," &c. 3 vols.
"Pure in tone and abounding in incident, this novel deserves warm commen-
dation."—*Morning Post.*
"The characters are well drawn, and have the merit of being exceedingly
natural."—*Guardian.*

GAYTHORNE HALL. By John M. Fothergill.
3 vols.
"The author has produced a good story, in which are found several characters
that show marked individuality."—*Morning Post.*
"'Gaythorne Hall' treats of a period of fierce political and social struggle in
a style replete with instruction and fascination."—*Newcastle Chronicle.*